# Salvation

Gina Clinton

# Contents

# 00 - Prologue - Ambrose Grayson's Point Of View.

------------------------------------------------------------

Stepping out of my ambulance, there was no sign of the bleeding man that had been called in. My partner, Mia, crossed her arms and huffed."This smells of mafia shit. Watch your ass, Grayson."

"I just want to make sure we aren't leaving someone behind. You hear me?"

"Watch your ass."

Grabbing my bag, I headed for the alley. There was a visible blood trail. It was still fresh, too. There was a possibility that there was something or rather someone there that needed our, or rather my, help.

"Mia, I've got--"Someone slapped their hand over my mouth and their other arm around my neck. Panic set in and I flailed in their arms.

"Move a fucking inch and I'll make sure you have a nice nap." He growled, his accent clearly Italian.

"Let-go-I'm a-medic," I said, to the best of my ability. He was crushing my windpipe. He roughly reached into my pockets and I felt him yank out my wallet before.

"Ambrose Grayson..." He muttered before he tightened his grip even more. The sound of someone rushing over was all that kept me awake.

"Let go of him! Goddamn it! You're going to get us into so much fucking trouble. That is my chief's only fucking son, Di Salvo."

The sound was familiar, and the man loosened his grip and another set of hands held me up.

"Ambrose, can you hear me? Fucking say something?"

"Ugh." I grunted, finally getting a look at my saviour. Sasha fucking Dean. This was definitely mafia bullshit. The other man slinked away into the dark, his figure large and his face, or what I saw of it, horribly handsome.

"Let me help you."

"I'm fine."

"You can barely hold yourself up."

"I just need to catch a few breaths and I'll be fine."

"What the hell were you doing here?" He hissed.

"We got a call. I figured it was Mafia related, but I didn't expect this. Just who the fuck was that guy?" I said, rubbing my throat.

"I can't discuss that with you."

"Of fucking course you can't, but I'm damn sure my dad knows who that hell he is?"

"Of course he does, he's the chief of police-"

"He's a dirty cop." I grunted. Looking at Sasha. He looked good. But he did every time I saw him. His lover was good for him, mafia or not.

"Let me help you back to the bus. I'll make something up and---"

"Fine. But make it good. Fuck."

Sasha took my bag and helped me back to the ambulance. Mia got out when she saw me and started freaking out.

"I fucking told you this was mafia shit. I told you to watch your ass. But no. And just who the hell are you?" She snapped, her eyes narrowing on Sasha.

"Sasha Dean. Officer. Want to see my badge?"

"That true, Grayson?"

"Yeah, he's a sheep of my father's flock."

"That's polite. Maybe next time I'll let the creep in the alley use you as a stress ball." Sasha said flatly.

"I've got him." Mia said, yanking me to the back of the bus and opened the door, shoving me and the bag inside before slamming the doors shut in Sasha's face.

"Grayson. What the hell man, you look like someone tried to end you. You need to go to the ER. I'm calling dispatch and taking you there."

"We have work to do. Just drive us back to the bay and I'll be fine by the time we get there."

"I hope you intend to file a report with the boss in case anything else happens. You know, later."

"Nothing is going to happen later. Seriously. It was a one-off thing."

She sighed. But nodded. "Just know I don't believe you, Ambrose."

"That's fine."

Mia drove back to the ambulance bay, and after she explained the whole situation to our boss against my wishes, they sent me home, or rather. Told to go file a report with my father and then go to the ER to get looked after. That honestly didn't feel like it needed to happen. But here I was. Pulling into the station and getting out. Tucking my keys in my pocket. I remembered my wallet and checked my pockets. Finding it right where it had been before.

Pulling it out as I headed inside, everything looked like it had before, minus the fact my old student card was missing. It must have fallen out when he had pulled my wallet open. It was just a useless hunk of plastic. I just kept it in there for something to take up the empty space.

Lukas was waiting by the door when I got inside, camera in hand.

"Holy shit, you actually came. Haha."

"Taking bets on me?"

"Maybe the chief was worried you wouldn't actually come and report your attack. Though Sasha made a report too."

"Did he?"

"Yeah, he said some creep attacked you in the alley. He saw you and saved your life."

"Yeah. A Mafia creep." I grunted.

"Trust me, this will get dealt with."

"Yeah. I'm not too worried. I'm still breathing." I said, touching my throat.

"Your dad wanted me to take pictures before you head in to speak with him."

"Ok."

Stepping into another room, he took a bunch of pictures before he all but sent me off to my dad's office. My dad looked at my neck and sighed.

"How are you feeling?"

"Like a rag doll. But I'm fine. Sasha saved my ass."

"I'm going to have a talk with Maddox about this, or rather, one of the underbosses, and we will get this sorted out in a timely manner."

"Don't bother. Pretty sure he's not---"

"I'm doing it, regardless."

"I spoke with your boss and he assured me you're on medical leave for a week or two until your throat doesn't look like they nearly killed you."

"I didn't ask for that. I don't actually want medical leave. I want to work--"

"Sorry, but protocol is protocol. So you best head to the ER and get checked out. Report all damages to me, no matter how small." My father said, crossing his arms and making his point known.

"I'm fine, I don't need---"

"Better yet, let me call in a favour and get you looked at right now." He said, before pulling out his personal cell and calling a number.

"That's really not---"

"I wasn't asking you what you thought. I was telling you what the plan was, so you don't run off like you do, so sit put." He said. Before whoever he had called, picked up, and he spoke. I tuned him out, not at all interested in whoever he was discussing my health and wellbeing. I didn't know everyone that my father did, but I knew some of the larger players. I had a clue who he was calling. Alessio Mihail, son of Andrei and he was a large player. I knew enough about him and his family not to get in the way.

My father crossed his arms once he was off the phone, and spoke.

"Someone is coming to get you. Be on your very best behaviour on the way there. I mean it."

"Yeah, Yeah. I got it. You don't have to remind me not to flirt with the hands of death. I've already done that once this week, hell once today," I bitched.

I waited around until Sasha seemed to appear out of thin air.

"We meet again, Ambrose." Sasha said, chuckling.

"Yeah, I didn't think it would be you, though. That was coming to get me. I assumed it would be a grunt."

"Yeah, it might have been, if I hadn't offered first. Better it be someone you know taking you to see Alessio."

He pulled me along behind him, leaving my vehicle at the station. He told me not to worry about my car, someone would bring me back. I frowned at the idea, and was just going to tell him it was fine and to let me go home, but he spoke.

"Ambrose, not a good idea. Alessio is waiting for you, and you don't want to waste his time. Trust me."

Sighing deeply, I got into his SUV and buckled in.

"Who was it earlier that tried to end me?" I asked, again.

"As I told you, Ambrose, I can't tell you that information. But know that I am dealing with it."

"Fine." I said flatly before mentioning that I was missing my school card, and that if they found it, I would like it back.

"We didn't, but if they do find it, you will be the first to know, of course."

"I doubt that. But thanks anyway."

"Look, I know this is a lot. Trust me on that. But I am going to make sure that what he did to you is brought up and punished. There was no reason for it. You were just doing your job."

"Yeah, I could have ignored the call, but if someone died because of me, it would be my ass. Not anyone else's, and I couldn't do that to someone, Mafia or not."

"I get it, trust me Ambrose."

# 01 - Chapter One - Ambrose Grayson's Point Of View.

----------------------------------------

The complex, as Sasha called it, rolled into view, and he stopped at the gate. He spoke in what I assumed was broken Italian before heading into the courtyard area at the front of the house. He parked and got out first.

"Come on, you're safe. I swear."

"I want to believe you, but I'm pretty sure the man responsible for this is here." I said, gesturing to my neck. He sighed. "You're not wrong. He is here, but you're not going anywhere near him. Trust me on that."

I closed my mouth before I said the words on my tongue and followed close to Sasha as he headed inside. It was way busier inside than I figured it would be. All kinds of conversations flooded into my ears, from laughing to shouting. He set his hand on my upper back and directed me through the house, down a set of stairs and down another set of halls. It was getting confusing quickly.

"How the hell do you live here? I would get lost just trying to get to and from work."

"You get used to it after some time."

"I would never."

He scanned his phone on the front of the pad and the metal doors popped open, the lock clicking. He lightly pushed me inside and called out for Alessio.

"I'm right here Sasha. Just give me a moment to finish up here."

"Take your time. We can wait."

Sasha turned to me and spoke.

"The man who did that to you isn't one of Maddox's men. He is kind of on loan, per se. That's why even if I wanted to tell who it was that did this to you, I can't."

"Hey, don't worry. I get it."

Alessio, the perfect image of his father, stepped into view, his glasses resting on his forehead and not the bridge of his nose. He pulled them down and whistled.

"Look at that. Fuck, he got you good. That's going to bruise like crazy."

"I figured that."

Sasha's phone rang, and he fetched it from his pocket and held it to his ear. I could hear the yelling from where I was.

"Alessio, Ambrose might have to wait for a few minutes. Luca and Marco have gotten physical. I need to get up there and get this under control."

"Go, Go, I've got this."

The younger doctor sighed.

"You have no idea the shit I deal with around here from these walking anger issues."

"I could never."

"It's different when you grow up in the heat of it, versus outside it."

"I bet——--" Crashing sounds and more cut me off as Alessio yanked me out of the way of two large men clearing going at it. They were interested in ripping each other apart.

"Luca, Stand down!" Alessio said sharply. The one male did exactly that, but not before he gave one last punch. Sasha and another man, this one far larger than the rest, his eyes scary cold.

The other man dusted himself off, looking at Alessio, and our eyes met. I realized was the man from before, the one who choked me.

"What the hell is going on here?" Alessio demanded with the air of authority.

"He was running his fucking mouth, and he got what——--"

"Please, I was just reminding you I had him before——--"

"Shut your fucking mouth."

"Make me, or are you too scared your boss with hang you out to——-"

"Marco! Enough!" Sasha demanded.

Marco, huh? I had a first name for the face of the man, at least now. Our eyes met again. I tore my eyes off him and looked at Sasha.

"Sorry it's not usually like this." Alessio grumbled.

Both males were bleeding, Split lips, bloody noses, and black eyes, those were for sure the outcomes here. Alessio checked on the one male, not the one who attacked me, and left the other male there. Groaning, unable to turn my healthcare brain off, I yanked on a pair of gloves from the wall holder where Alessio had and slipped them on.

"Ambrose, Wait."

Sasha grabbed my upper arm.

"Don't let me try to kill me again, yeah?"

"This isn't wise."

"He needs to stop that from bleeding, and I have some knowledge there. Let me at least use it. He might try to kill me less."

"I don't like this idea. I wish you would listen."

"Healthcare brain, I help where I am needed."

Sasha shoved a few gauze pads and a box of wipes into my hands.

"For the love of god, don't tell your dad I let you do this shit." Sasha hissed.

I approached the man, Marco. He had a tissue pressed to his split lip and was pinching his nose. He was clearly fuming about this whole fight. Holding the wipes and gauze in my hands to show that I can in peace, he seemed to let me get closer.

"What do you want?" He said, his voice muffled.

"To help with your wounds."

"Why? What reason do you have?" He hissed, holding his wounds still.

"Put your hands down and let me see your wounds, so that I can appropriately dress them as needed." I muttered.

He lowered his voice to a whisper before he spoke again.

"Not worried I might choke you again?"

"Maybe if you decide to choke me again, do it in a way we will both like." I said, using humour to try not to show him how much I was actually worried about him hurting me again. His eyes scanned me this time, and he dropped his hands, and blood poured freely from his nose and the split lip. I pinched his nose right away and had him lean forward.

"Hold this to your nose, and pinch, lean forward too." I said.

As he did that, I pressed gauze to his lip, and he cursed me out in both English and Italian. I would have found it amusing if he hadn't tried to murder me this early afternoon. Alessio came and took over from me after he got a fresh pair of gloves and the whole time he seemed to chew out the other male in Italian. I was glad I wasn't him. Alessio was pissed. Two more guys came and then Maddox made himself known. He met eyes with me as I was pulling off the gloves and he smiled tightly, nodding, his eyes scanning my neck.

It had been a good while since I had seen Maddox, but he looked happy and healthy. He stopped in front of the two of them and crossed his arms.

"So who wants to tell me what the fuck happened here? Make it quick. I'm losing my patience."

"He started it." Marco grunted, which earned a sound of disgust from the other man, Luca. Another man, smaller, but definitely in the Vincent family blood pool, crossed his arms in annoyance, leaning down and hissing in the man's ear.

"You both had been getting along with no problems. For Christ's sake, you were being civil."

"That was before he started trying to play off with your head with our fucking cities paramedics." Luca, I believe his name was, said harshly.

"I told you it was a mistake, and you brought up my previous relationship, one I would like to stay in the past for both of our sakes. You don't like me, but I keep telling you and him I didn't do this all purposely. I didn't even know his fucking daughter existed. I am just trying to make the best situation out of what they presented and I am far from fucking perfect. I am actively trying to better—-"

"Oh, can it whinny. With this, I'm turning my life around bullshit. You're a snake, and you can't fool me." The other man snapped.

Alessio sighed, and took came over, lightly pulling me into a side room, an office and closing the door, not that it did much to help. It was a very heated discussion outside.

"They really don't seem to like each other."

"You can say that again. It's a really messy situation, but everyone is trying, or at least trying sometimes, to make the best out of it. Luca is a hothead. He means well though ninety per cent of the time. It just gets ugly when you are in the situation where they are. Ex-husband versus current. Luca has a very unhappy opinion about Marco. But I can't blame him. There were a lot of terrible things in that marriage before. Sorry, I should just dump all this on you." He chuckled.

"I don't know either of them, so I can't pass judgement on them. But you can feel their dislike for each other in the air." I said.

My only interaction with the other man, Marco, was not a pleasant one before this, and it seemed like it was pretty well known.

"Alright, let me look at your neck and we can get you out of this circus and back home."

"Thank you, I appreciate that."

He had me pull off the uniform top, and he pulled on gloves, and inspected my neck, humming. He touched a spot on my neck before checking all the bones, making sure they all moved and functioned the proper way.

"Plenty of soft tissue damage. You're going to be bruised for a few weeks. It's already setting in. I would recommend monitoring the bruises and if anything else pops up, call me and I'll check it out right away."

He grabbed a piece of paper and jotted down a number before handing it over.

"Thank you."

"You're welcome. I really don't mind. Pretty glad the chief called to have me check up on you. I was wondering if you were alright when I was informed about what happened." Alessio said, sliding his glasses up again, massaging the bridge of his nose before sliding them back down.

Alessio walked me out to Sasha and gave him the all clear to take me home, and I glanced back at the situation behind us. Meeting eyes with Marco again, I frowned, tearing my eyes off his and following behind Sasha.

# 02 - Chapter Two - Ambrose Grayson's Point Of View.

--------------------------------------------------

Crossing my arms and looking at my boss, I thought he was actually joking, but that wasn't the case here.

"Ambrose I'm being serious, until the Mafia is done fighting with the new gangs in our area, Mia and you will work out of the next town over. This is the safest thing to do."

"What about the others? Are they not being——-"

"Their fathers aren't the chief of police. You know you're a special case, Ambrose."

"This is utter bullshit. I can't just pick up all my shit and move it to the next town over!" I yelled in frustration.

"Yes, you can, and you will if you intend to keep your job. You will start there next Friday. That gives you ten days to find accommodations in the area. Mia has already agreed and is looking for a place. Reach out to her and maybe she can help you."

Biting back the words on my tongue, I left the bay. Yes, I would get a relocation bonus, but this was still bullshit. I served my two weeks off for this? I slammed my car door as I got back in, heading towards dad's. This was all his fault, and I was going to let him know that.

Pulling into the driveway, his car was there, but so was Maddox's. Based on the time, they were having a dinner meeting here. The neighbours were unaware of how close the mafia boss was to them. This was a private, normal looking car. He always showed up in this one when he came here, otherwise it was flashy sports cars and SUVs. I let myself in, like I still lived here. I barely registered the gun pointed at me. This was one of the five underbosses. I didn't know him well, but he knew me.

"Sorry, did not know you were going to be showing up." He said, tucking away his weapon.

"Neither did I." I grumbled, not bothering to take my shoes off when he let me pass.

Maddox and my dad were speaking about safety measures and I cleared my throat before pulling out a chair. I waited until Maddox finished speaking before I interrupted. I was mad, not stupid.

"You and I need to have some words. For you to go over my head and make choices for me is bullshit. I have grown up here, and worked here for a long ass time. You just don't get to do this shit." I snapped, looking at my father, making it clear it was him I was annoyed with.

"They suggested it to me, and I happened to say it was a good idea. Simmer down, Ambrose."

"Simmer down.. You did not actually just say that to me?" I said, looking at him, almost dumbfounded. I chuckled before looking at Maddox.

"Excuse my actions." I muttered, before picking up the centrepiece on the table, setting the flowers on the top, and tossing the water in it at my father.

"Ambrose!" He yelled, pissed off that I drenched him.

"What? Don't like it when someone takes your choice away, huh? Kind of like I just took away your choice of being dry."

"This is my house—--"

"This is my mother's house, actually." I muttered, setting the vase back down and putting the flowers back in it, and reaching across the table to take the glass of water my father was drinking and refilling the vase.

I looked back to Maddox and then back to my father.

"Have a splendid dinner. Bye."

"Ambrose, we are not done here." My father said, standing up.

"Oh, we are. I have ten fucking days to find a new place to live in the next city over, since I have to work there now, since someone like to piss around in my affairs."

"Ambrose!" He yelled.

I turned around and chuckled.

"Oh, and don't forget to tell my mother about this."

Leaving, I slammed the door on my way out. I was still pissed off and fuming about this whole fucking deal. I should have gone home, but I really didn't want to deal with that right now. Instead, here I was, outside of the bar at eight pm. I had a drink every now and again here after some long shifts. The bartender looked at me when I walked inside.

"Ambrose, you're early, not working tonight?"

"Oh boy, that's a loaded question."

"Tell me about it, but first, you intend on getting heavy with the bottle tonight?"

"Perhaps, Here I know what you want."

I tossed him my keys. He wrapped a paper label around the loop and wrote my name on it, and dropped them in the key bucket for the night. He slid an empty glass in front of me and spoke as he poured.

"Tell me about your troubles, Grayson."

"Ugh, where the fuck do I start?"

"The beginning is the best spot, normally." He laughed.

I tipped the glass back and felt the burn of the whiskey as it went down. Setting it down, I pulled out my wallet and dropped two hundred on the top of the bar.

"One of those nights, huh?"

"It's going to be."

"I'm glad I took your keys, then."

"You and I both."

I started rattling on about my last few weeks and then about the shit I walked into at work today and my father's decision to move me to a different city without my approval.

"I can see how that would be frustrating. Your father makes a ton of choices for you, and his power is well known, for many reasons."

"Besides that, he's in the pocket of you know who, he's got no power without him. Sort of." I groaned.

I was all too aware that this was a Mafia owned place, but what family owned it, was the question. Maddox had been allowing some of the other families to have business here, as long as they respected his territory and didn't cause problems. Friends of his, you could say, if he even had friends.

Tossing back a second drink, I was still annoyed. The bartender was being pretty heavy-handed tonight and not really watching my alcohol consumption, and I knew it. By around ten pm, the bar was pretty full, and I was a few drinks deep.

One thing led to another, and it was hard to tell what actually started the fight behind me, but even I was eventually pulled into it. A bartender was on the phone. The mafia was going to be crawling all over this place in a minute, but that didn't stop people from throwing hands. The bartender yanked me out of the way before I got crushed by people fighting.

"Stay here. You are too drunk to be that close to this shit. Besides, they are on their way." He said.

"Who owns this?" I muttered, not really thinking about it, and not really hearing more than the words 'Di Salvo'. I couldn't figure out where the hell I had heard that before.

Minutes later, the bar was being commanded by a few taller males, guns clearly on their hips. They spoke to the bartender, and he nodded before speaking.

"Attention ladies and gentlemen. The owner is on his way and not a single one of you is to leave the bar until he dismisses all of you. Destruction of property and such, you know."

The bartender gave me the open bottle.

"Amuse yourself Ambrose, it's going to be a long fucking night."

"Right. Well, I should try to get sober then. In case I need to walk or some shit." I groaned.

I pulled out my phone, debating texting someone for a hand, but honestly, the only person I had from the Mafia was Alessio and I would not beg him for help. I had nothing to do with the fight, so I was going to be just fine. The few men cleaned up some tables and chairs, having everyone sit back down, quietly. The bartender let me go back to my chair where I had been.

He passed me a glass of water and spoke.

"Should help you sober up a little."

"Right, thanks."

Drinking it back, I looked at the doors when they opened and he walked in. I could have puked my guts out right then and there. It was the fucking guy from the complex and the one tried to pop my damn head off nearly. Marco.

I really was not sober enough for this.

"Any chance I could sneak out the back?" I muttered.

"No. Marco would make sure you were found."

"Ha, that's the thing I'm worried about."

"Marco is only interested in those who wrecked his bar——-"

"He is the one who choked me in the alley." I muttered, drinking the rest of the water and praying to sober up quicker. Marco commanded the bar and started forcing everyone to piece together the events that happened. I watched him speaking and moving around from the mirror over the top of the bar. Once he let the others leave, I tried to sneak out, but he snagged my arm.

"Hold up. Not you, I haven't had the chance to ask you about what you—--" He spun me around. "Oh. It's you." He muttered, frowning.

"I'm loaded and would like to go home." I said, trying to pull my arm out of his grip.

"Yeah, I don't think so. We need to have a long conversation about not only what you saw tonight while in the bar, but also about the alley incident."

"I didn't see shit, and I don't know shit. As for you choking me all unsexy like, I'm not in interested in reliving that, thanks but no thanks."

"Right, so that's not how this is going to work. We are going to speak about what happened."

"Yeah, I will pass." I hissed.

"You don't get that option. At least, at this moment." He said.

"Give me my damn keys so I can go the fuck home." I snapped at the bartender.

"Do not. He is drunk and I can drive him home." Marco said.

"Driving drunk is far better than getting into a car with you. You tried to kill me!"

"Hardly. I tried to make you pass out, not kill you."

"Keys. Now."

"No, I will not let you drive drunk."

"Fine. Then Ill just fucking walk."

"That's dangerous."

"I'll take my chances—--" He pulled me out of the bar behind him "Hey wait!"

He shoved me in the side of his SUV and closed the door. He got in on the other side and demanded I put my seatbelt on. Not trusting him, I did just that. He waited before he started driving.

"Where am I taking you?" He asked.

"To my death?" I muttered.

"Hardly. Where do you live so I can take you home?"

"Oh, right?" I gave him the directions, but when I reached for my keys I hissed.

"I can't get inside."

"What, why?"

"My keys."

"Guess you're coming with me then."

"What! No, I can stay at my dad's—-"

"It's one in the morning. Just give it a rest and I'll drive you back in the morning."

"Fine. But you better."

"You have my word."

# 03 - Chapter Three - Ambrose Grayson's Point Of View.

------------------------------------------------------------

Stretching out, the sound of a baby crying made all the events from last night flood right back in. I was in the enemy's home. I went home with him last night, because I couldn't get into my apartment. He was speaking and I could hear him walking, too.

"You mustn't yell, Amore Mio, you will wake up our house guest, and he was unwilling last night. He will probably have a hangover, and your cries will be like glass in his ears."

He was right. I had a hangover, but not that bad. Thank the heavens for that. The clock on the nightstand in the spare room he lent said it was six in the morning. The baby stopped crying, and I heard him still walking around. I did not know a man like this would have a baby. He must have had a wife, too. I wondered what she would think about me being here.

Standing up, I used the attached bathroom, then opened the bedroom door. He was walking around the living room with a small sleeping baby in his arms.

"Sorry, I hope we didn't wake you." He whispered.

"No. Even if you did, it's not like I can be upset about it. Please apologize to your wife for needing to stay here last night."

"My wife? I'm sorry, I think you're confused. I am not married, nor do I have a wife. When I was married, it was to a man." He said.

"Oh."

"It was my son, right? That's why you thought I had a wife?"

"Honestly, yes."

"That's fair. I get it."

I nodded, pinching the bridge of my nose, trying to stop the throbbing in my head.

"Let me just put him down and I'll get you something for the headache." He whispered.

"Alright."

He set the baby down in a swing and left. I watched the swing rock the baby back and forth. He was cute. Even in the low light out here, you could see that this child was biologically his. He cleared his throat, a water bottle in his hand and a bottle of painkillers in the other.

"They are both new, in case you don't trust me."

"Thanks."

I took the bottle and cracked the lid off; he opened the painkillers and handed me two. He dropped them in my open hand and I tossed them in my mouth and then took a sip of water. Swallowing them down, he hummed.

"You should eat something small with those. So they don't give you a stomachache."

"Probably."

"Come, I'll make you something small."

"That's really unnecessary."

"Please, let me. It's the least I can do after what I did to you in the alley, and after you still helped me at Maddox's."

"Fine. But understand, I'm not big on you Mafia men."

"Understood."

I watched as he cooked something small in the kitchen.

"Is the baby ok there by himself?"

"Wren will be fine. And I have this."

He pulled up the side of his shirt and tucked into his waistband was a baby monitor.

"So, you said you were married? What happened there?"

"For someone who doesn't like Mafia men, you surely have a lot of questions."

"Hmm, Yeah, Know your enemy and all that shit."

"Enemy? We are hardly that."

"My throat two weeks ago would disagree with you heavily."

"Yes. It would."

"What happened to your marriage?"

"The same thing that happened to your neck."

"That's vague."

"Sit, eat." He passed me a plate of food. "I will tell you about my marriage while you eat."

"You're actually going to tell me?" I said, mildly shocked.

"Yes. I have come to terms with my demons, at least there." He muttered, guilt in his eyes for a moment.

"I abused my ex-husband. I took my anger out on him. Things got too out of control for either of us. That entire glass house came down on us both."

I glanced at the living room where the child was, and he looked down.

"I know what you're thinking, that I will hurt him, too. But I would never. I was worried about that too, you know. I have actively been going for—--"

"You don't need to tell me this. It's private."

"Yes, it was private. But I showed you some of that anger in the alley when I thought a stranger might have discovered us. I acted without thinking it over. If Maddox's fifth underboss, Sasha, had not been there, you might actually be dead."

I swallowed the bite in my mouth, and it sank like lead.

"I see."

"I will take you home after you have finished eating and my boss comes to watch Wren for me."

"Actually. While we are here. I am being moved to this town for work, my father and Maddox's doing, I assume. After the incident with you. I need to find a place to rent and I have ten days to do so. Do you know anything that might be available?"

"I don't, but I can find out if you would like me to? I understand if you would like to limit the contact with how things have turned out this far with us."

"Keep your hands to yourself, and I don't mind. But I won't be involved in Mafia violence or issues, and if you touch me again, the way you did in that alleyway, I will have you arrested. Knowing this, I don't care if my father is in Maddox's pocket or not. He won't be enough to save you."

"I understand." A soft smile tugged at his lips, as if I didn't just openly threaten him in his own home after he was nice enough to offer me a place last night. He walked to another room, and came back with something in his hands a moment later, setting it on the table.

My student card looked back at me.

"You know I knew you had this, right?"

"Did you?"

"Yes, I noticed it missing and Sasha said they didn't find it in the alley. So then, I must know, why did you take it? Some kind of trophy?"

He looked offended. Frowning before he spoke again.

"No. Not even close. I took something you wouldn't need so that I could look into you. That is all."

"You have a strange—-"

"Also, you are an unruly drunk. Might I add. You bit me last night when I tried to help you stand up, when you fell in the grass."

"I bit you—I don't believe you."

"I have proof, besides the teeth marks."

"Prove it!" I raised my voice, embarrassed.

He peeled off this sweater, his shirt underneath riding up and giving me a really delightful view of his deeply tanned skin. He stuck his arm out, and true to his words, he had a bruised set of teeth marks.

"I also have it on video, if you would like to see that as well."

"No, thank you." I muttered.

"Back to my marriage for a moment. My ex left, and it was the best thing he could have done for both of us. I was bitter at first, but I understand he is both happier and healthier away from me. We do not work well together, even for a short time period."

"At least you can understand that. Not everyone can."

"Understanding the damage I've done to him is the least I can do. Changing my behaviours is something I need to do, for both myself and my son."

I nodded again, standing up and taking my dish to the sink.

"Pass me your dish and I'll wash—-" I turned around, and he was far too close to me "---It"

"Sorry, here. You don't have to, I can do that—-"

"I have it. Just give me the plate."

He let go of the plate when I grabbed onto it and I washed up the few dishes quickly and tried to dry my hands on my shirt.

"Here, towel."

I took it and dried my hands before passing it back to him. The sound of someone else coming into the house had me frozen in place.

"Ah, My boss is here."

I nodded. Unsure of who and what was about to come into the kitchen doorway. A taller man entered the kitchen and paused.

"Oh, I'm sorry. I was unaware you had company, Marco." His thick Italian accent made it harder to understand his words, but he spoke slowly.

"This is Ambrose Grayson."

"Pleasure to meet you, Ambrose." He nodded, cast his eyes at Marco, and it said everything his words did not. He wanted to know who I was and what I was doing here.

"Likewise." I said politely.

"Are you by chance related to the Chief of police, Ambrose?"

"Yes, He's my father."

"How delightful. He's a very nice guy."

"I suppose that depends on how you look at him." I muttered without thinking about who I was in the presence of.

"Not a fan of your father or of his friends?" He asked.

Marco intercepted.

"Romeao, I'm sure Ambrose is a busy guy."

"Marco, I asked him a question. Now, close your mouth."

Marco nodded.

"I'm not a fan of the Mafia, if that's what you're asking. Though I will be respectful when and where it matters. I don't get involved in the affairs of the Mafia."

"I see you're a smart man."

"I try to be."

"If I am to be honest, I prefer to be in the company of those who like me for my behaviour, not my money and power." Romeao, Marco's boss, said, smiling at me.

Marco gave him the baby monitor and said something in Italian before he looked at me.

"I hope to see you around, Ambrose Grayson."

"You too."

Marco helped me gather all my things from the night before and when we got into his SUV, he apologized for his bosses behaviour.

"I think he's a decent guy, actually." I muttered.

# 04 - Chapter Four - Ambrose Grayson's Point Of View.

-------------------------------------------------------------

Packing up boxes, I had a week to find something. Mia had found a place right away that would take her. We both had been looking for me, but nothing was coming up that was decent. I was growing frustrated with the whole deal. Dad had called to speak to me after finding out from a friend that someone had spotted me with Marco. It was more like he was trying to get information from me and I wasn't doing it. I shut him down right away, telling him it wasn't important.

Marco and I had exchanged phone numbers in case he came across something, a rental I could get last minute. Mia had mentioned I could come stay with her until I found something, but I couldn't do that. I wanted my space.

Getting a hotel was an option, but it would be expensive and I would have to put my things into storage. Running my hands through my hair, I sighed. I had to figure something out quickly.

Checking my phone, I had a text from Marco. I hadn't intended to actually answer him, but I accidentally hit the phone button, and he picked up before I could hang up.

"Hello, Did you see the text I sent you?"

"Oh, Yeah, I did." I had not. I didn't have time before my blunder.

"Right, so Romeao said you're welcome to an apartment in the complex he owns, but I don't think it's a safe option."

"I need it, Marco. Safe or not." I hissed with frustration, heavy in my voice.

"I'll take you to see the place, but I don't think it's a wise idea, Ambrose."

"I get that, but I need it. I can always find something later."

"I can take you to see the place tomorrow then, I just need to get Romeao to watch—-"

"Just bring him, unless it's a safety thing." I muttered. I wanted to see his little one again. He was cute.

"Are you sure?"

"Yeah, your son doesn't bother me in the slightest. I'm used to kids." I said, stating the truth. I have been around so many kids now with my profession.

"If you're alright with it, then I will bring Wren. I don't see it being dangerous for him."

"Don't put off spending time with your child for my comfort." I said, being serious. I could only imagine he was used to having to find someone to watch his son often.

"Alright."

He hung up then, and I glanced around my apartment, still feeling like I was going to pull my hair out. I bought boxes when I got my car back from the bar, and yet here they were, still empty and not even folded. I didn't even know where to start. It was a lot of work. I hadn't even given my notice yet, because I was worried about not finding another place. I hoped that this place Marco had suggested was going to work, even for a short time. Just until I could find something better. Otherwise, I was royally fucked.

Taking a few of the boxes, I headed into the kitchen and started packing away anything I really didn't use, which was ninety per cent of everything I owned. I didn't have the time or energy to cook most times after work. I worked a lot of overtime so that I could have extra cash for fun things and times.

By the time I actually get back to work, I will have missed nearly a damn month of work and overtime pay. That was a lot of money I could use. The bonus was the only reason I was doing this. I needed the bonus now.

Hunting through the house, I finally found a permanent marker to mark the box as unused kitchen junk. Looking around the kitchen at all the rest of the things I owned, from the fancy coffee maker to the computer on my island. This place has been my home for the last eight years. My entire life and career were here.

Sighing, I couldn't believe I had been doing this career choice for eight years. The things I had learned from twenty to twenty-eight were astounding. I had also unfortunately confronted both death and the limits of the human body.

Folding another box up, I loaded it full of plastic containers, cups, and plates. I had long given up on glass plates and cups. Plastic was just cheaper to replace in the end, and harder to break.

By midnight, I packed up most of the kitchen and some of the living room. I was going to need many more boxes just for the living room. My apartment was looking like a shell of its former self. Shaking off the sleep that crept in, I had one more box in the living room I wanted to pack up before heading to bed. Carefully stacking my books in the box, I was careful to make sure they wouldn't get bent or torn before closing the box. Marking the box, I closed it up and sighed as flicking the kitchen light off. Laying down on the couch, I was hungry again, but I was far too exhausted to make anything.

Sitting up with a start, the sound of banging on my door had me tripping over my feet to get to the door to make the sound stop. Yanking open the door, my father stood there, looking unamused.

"Did you just get up? It's noon, Ambrose."

"Hi to you too. I had a long night packing up my apartment. What are you doing here?"

"You've been ignoring my texts and calls, and when we spoke, you were ignoring my questions."

"Your questions were about Marco and why I was seen with him. Which, by the way, isn't your business. I'm a grown ass man." I muttered, closing the door now that he had come inside.

"I'm your father. Your business is my business, Ambrose. Even more so when it comes to Marco Di Salvo. He is a dangerous man with a vio-lent——-"

"I am aware. Pretty fucking aware, thank you." I hissed.

"You know about what he did to his ex-husband, then?"

"He told me about his past, and his ex husband all on his own. So yes, I know some of it, probably not all of it. But I don't care to hear his dirty laundry from you."

"Ambrose he could—-"

"Need I remind you that cops are far from perfect too? They hurt people—-"

"Enough."

"So it's only fine to bring up violence when it's the mafia. Got it." I hissed, annoyed with his two-sided behaviour.

"It's not like that. But we don't need to argue about that subject right now. I want to know why the hell they saw you with Marco. If he did something to you, you need to tell me right now. I can make sure whatever the reason is, is dealt with."

"There is no reason other than he is being far more helpful than you've been, honestly."

"Ambrose, he choked you! How can you actively be around him? He's dangerous?"

"We have an understanding right now."

"And that is?"

"That is none of your business. And even if it was, I still wouldn't tell you." I said flatly, looking right at him. His face instantly showed his dislike of the comment I made.

"You're going to wind up dead somewhere because of this attitude of yours towards all this shit."

"Says the man who takes bribes from mafia men. But hey, continue on, I guess." I sighed, heading to make a cup of coffee. "Want coffee?"

"If that's alright with you, then yes."

"Wouldn't offer it if it wasn't." I replied, dropping a single serve coffee in the coffeemaker and closing the lid before placing the one of the two coffee cups I left out under neath. Hitting the button, I wanted for the very pleasing hiss sound to show that this coffee was done. Removing the one cup, I tucked the other underneath and repeated the steps from before. Setting the coffee on the counter, looking at dad.

"Here, coffee is done. Milk, cream and sugar are in the same places for now. Help yourself."

"Thank you. And as much as you hate it, moving isn't a bad thing. You will be free from most of the mafia around here, minus a few here and there. Marco, being one."

"What about the family Marco is from? They must not be that far."

"Romeao's family is outside of our district and that town's limits. It's about a half hour drive from his 'home' to where you will be in town."

"Marco lives in the city. Nice place." I muttered.

"I said there were a few." My dad said as he took a sip of his coffee.

Grabbing ice cubes out of the freezer, I dropped them into a fresh cup and poured cream in the cup before adding the hot coffee. Ice coffee was exactly what I needed to deal with him right now. And Marco, later.

I was waiting for Marco to text or call and say he was ready to show me the apartment. If I actually took the place, and chances were, I would. My dad was going to lose his ever loving mind.

"Your mother is pissed about this whole thing. The choking incident and the fact you're moving."

"Not by my choice."

"She is aware of that. She's just pissed because neither of us made her aware of the changes."

"Nothing for her is really changing, though. Honestly, she will still work long hours and travel for work all the time. We can still have that once a month large dinner that she needs to feel grounded here after coming home."

"Ambrose. Money is very important to your mother, you know this."

"Dad. I know, trust me. It was me, my entire teenage years, that listened to her complain about my marks and how she didn't come to this country to have a son who wastes his brain doing 'cosas tontas' (dumb things)."

"Your mother is your mother and you can't change her, Ambrose. She only wants what was best for you."

# 05 - Chapter Five - Ambrose Grayson's Point Of View.

---

**M**y dad got up to leave just as Marco texted me, saying he was on his way. My dad, seeing the message, sighed.

"Kid, listen ok. I don't care who or what you date, but if you end up with him, just please for the love of god. Be careful."

"Woah, it's really not like that, not even close."

"It doesn't take long for it to be like that, though, Ambrose."

"He's not my type."

"Thought you didn't have one. That's what you tell your mother, at least."

"Mafia men. They are a whole type that I don't do."

My father really didn't look convinced in the slightest, even though he knew my feelings about his dealings with the Mafia. They were decent people. I just didn't want to be involved or around them or their work. Yet here I was, going willingly with Marco.

"Time will tell if that's a rule you stick to"

"Goodbye to you too." I muttered, crossing my arms.

"I'll swing by and help you pack tomorrow, alright?"

"Yeah, sounds alright."

I couldn't actually believe my dad would put that out into the universe. If, on the slimmest chance it happened, he was fully to blame for putting that energy out there.

Finishing my watered down, once iced coffee, I jogged to the bedroom to find something to wear for the day. Pulling on some black jeans and a dark grey sweater, I hand combed my hair and slipped my feet into flip-flops. Annoyed with the way it was laying, I walked to the bathroom and wet it, before shaking it out with my fingers so that the waviness would be a little more tamed. Brushing my teeth, I paced the apartment before heading back and rinsing with mouthwash. Rinsing my toothbrush, I snapped the cover back in and placed it in the holder.

Marco called about ten minutes later to say he was just coming into town and would be here in the next five to ten minutes. Taking a deep breath, I double checked I had all my things. Once making sure I did, I left the apartment, keys in hand, and waited out front for Marco.

He pulled up a few minutes later, and I did a double take. The man was dressed down, wearing a leather jacket and jeans. He knew he was good looking, and he worked it.

"I hope this is a good time." He said, smiling softly.

"Yeah. Better now than earlier."

"Did something happen?"

"Not really, I passed out on the couch last night in a terrible position, woke up to my dad banging on the damn—I mean darn door and then he complained, which is normal honestly but yeah. He only left as you texted me." I groaned, buckling up my seat belt. Glancing in the backseat, Wren was there, and he was sawing logs.

"How long has he been out?"

"The entire ride. Car rides knock him out pretty quickly."

"Oh?"

"I spent many nights driving him around just so he would stay asleep."

"I could never do it on my own." I said before catching myself, "I personally just could never do it alone. I don't think I'm that responsible and for another life? Haha."

"I knew going into this I would do it alone, and there were some mistakes with his birth, and I'll never live those down, but I don't regret it."

"Mistakes? What do you mean?"

He explained the whole thing while he drove and honestly the whole deal sounded sketchy, but who was I to judge him when he very well could be telling the truth? I had no way of proving him wrong.

"Mistakes happen. At least he took it well."

"Yes, his partners did, too."

"Oh, yikes, partners, that makes it more complicated."

"Yes."

"I mean, if it helps, you made a cute kid." I said, looking back at Wren again.

"Thanks, I guess."

Quiet overtook the SUV, and it was torture for me. So I broke it.

"Did you get the bar fixed up?"

"Yes. The cameras were an enormous help, in part with first-person accounts."

"Ah. Yes, that would be helpful, and um... I'm sorry I bit you."

"Please, you are far from the first to bite me, but I appreciate the apology, nonetheless. I would say we are even, but that's not true." He hummed.

"If it never happens again, I will forget it ever happened."

"No. That's not ok, because it happened."

"Yes, I do not deny that. What I am saying is that if it never happens again, then there is no reason to keep bringing it up, Marco. A bad judgement call is just that, but it's not the end of the world. I am perfectly fine, and you have expressed that it was a bad call. That's the end of it." I replied, before checking my phone because it vibrated. It was Mia. She was letting me know she was working on moving her things into her new apartment.

"So tell me about the apartments?""Oh, right? So the apartments are owned by Romeao and we use them for coworkers, under me, that don't have places they own."

"Coworkers, you mean henchmen, right?"

"Yes, I figured you might prefer coworkers."

"I would prefer you not sugarcoat things for me, If I'm honest Marco. You give your men titles and I can handle them. I know a bit about the mafia, or at least Maddox's family."

"I will keep that in mind."

"Moving on. Is there anything I should know?"

"It's your standard apartment set up, clean and renovated. Most of the men living there work at night and sleep in the daytime."

"Perfect, we will have opposite work schedules. They work while I sleep and vice versa."

"Should work out fine, then."

"Yes, it should. But as for the rent payments? Do you know what Romaeo charges for the rent?"

"He mentioned something about discussing it over dinner, if you liked the apartment."

"Right, sounds good. Have a quick look around the place and then I can give you my answer about the apartment, but chances are I will take it."

"I will let him know your choice after you see the apartment." Marco replied.

He pulled into the driveway of an apartment building not too long after. If you didn't know it was mafia owned, there was nothing that gave it away. It was your typical apartment building, aside from the large stone sign with the building name and the words 'privately owned building' tacked on the bottom. Which still really didn't look out of the normal of this city.

Getting out first, he grabbed the baby, carrier and all.

"Would you like me to take him or help in some way?" I asked.

"Oh, no. I've got it, but thank you."

Wren opened his eyes and before he could even make some kind of noise, Marco popped a soother in his mouth. Marco used a keycard to let us into the building and I followed him since he seemed to know right where he was going.

"Stairs or elevator?" He asked.

"Whatever works best for you."

Tracking up the stairs, the man was fast, even with a baby and carrier. On the second floor, right in the middle of the hall, he used a key to open the door, and we stepped inside.

"Please, have a good look around." He said politely before pulling out his phone and texting someone. I walked from room to room and looked around at everything. True to his word, everything looked well maintained and clean. But it was also shockingly quiet.

Returning to Marco, I told him I would take it. He nodded.

"Let me just let Romeao know. I'm going to step into the hall. Can you watch him?"

"Oh sure, take your time."

I watched Marco leave and sat down on the wood floor beside the carrier and rocked it with my hand and not my foot like he had been doing. I wasn't that skilled, but also, I didn't want to get dirt or other junk particles on Wren or even close to him.

Wren opened his little eyes and his face scrunched up, before he spit that soother out and started the wail. Tucking the soother back into his mouth, he stopped screaming, but looked like he might start again. Against my better judgement, I took him out of the car seat and held him and his little blanket. He fit in the crook of my arm and any fussing he had been doing stopped. He was content, his little eyes looking up at me.

He sucked the soother and just watched me as I watched him. His eyes fluttered shut eventually. Whatever Marco was discussing, it was taking a while. I thought about tucking him back into the car seat, but I didn't want him to scream again.

Sitting with my legs crossed on the floor was how Marco found me when he returned, his sleeping son tucked into my chest and arm.

"Sorry he was crying and——"

"No worries. He looks just fine. Though he is probably going to get fussy soon because it's close to the time he eats lunch normally."

"Oh. We can head out so you can feed him."

"We can head from here to my home, and I'll feed him, then I can take you home."

"Alright, but I am in no rush, so please don't feel you need to rush me home."

"I just don't want to take up too much of you time while you need to pack and get ready to move things into the apartment."

"Did he say anything about the dinner to discuss the rent when you spoke to him?"

"Ah, yes. He said dinner would have to wait. But he is asking for one thousand a month, all-inclusive."

"Deal. I can easily afford that."

I tucked Wren back into the carrier as Marco texted Romeao to let him know it was a deal. Wren stayed sleeping, even as I buckled him in and covered him in the light blanket. Marco picked up the carrier, and we headed out.

# 06 - Chapter Six - Ambrose Grayson's Point Of View.

Marco got me set up with paying Romeao a few days later and got me the apartment key and the keycard for the building. I paid first and last month's rent, gave my notice on my current apartment and started moving boxes, with help from dad, Sasha and his partner, who only agreed because Sasha had. Having moved the last boxes the night before and my cat, I only had two days to really unpack things and get settled in the best I could before I had to head to work.

Marco had offered to lend a hand with the moving, but I suggested that he not try that. Mostly because of my dad. Marco was supposed to be coming later on today with a housewarming gift and lunch. The apartment was quiet right now in the daytime because all the henchmen were sleeping. Tonight, that was going to be the big tell all. When they were working and awake.

Moving a box of my clothing out of the way, I shoved a few boxes of crap I didn't want to unpack right now into the closet. Mochi mewed from the bed and looked at him.

"If you had thumbs, I would make you help too, you old man."

Mochi was seven, but actually acted like he was seventy. His white, sleek coat was soft and silky. He hadn't moved from the bed since I had got up, and honestly, if I didn't have the deadline of unpacking, I also would still be in bed.

Opening the box of my clothing, I stuffed it in the drawers of my dresser and hung up what needed to be. Looking at Mochi, I groaned.

"I dislike the Mafia, Mochi. I hate how much dad is in the pocket of Maddox, and his alliances. But, some of them... I guess they aren't all terrible people, you know? Haha, of course you don't, you're a cat. I guess what I mean is, Sasha, and his partner, and a handful of others, aren't bad. Just in a bad job field."

Mochi just meowed at me, and I felt for a moment like he at the very least understood me. Moving so that I could pet him, I continued rattling on.

"And him, who I don't want to speak about. I want to hate him and everything about him. But he's the one who's been the most helpful. Hell, without him, we wouldn't have this apartment right now. Again, you don't understand because you're a cat."

Checking my watch, I groaned. I needed to eat something small and get a cup of coffee before I could get the kitchen together more. So we had dishes and a table to have lunch at. Pants would also be another good idea. I had way too much skin showing to be comfortable when Marco actually showed up. While unpacking my things, I was trying to be as quiet as possible. I would feel terrible if I woke up the neighbours, knowing pretty much all of them worked nights. It made me wonder about Marco, though. Did he work all night long and look after Wren in the daytime?

I would cry.

Mochi followed me to the kitchen, singing the song of his people. I figured he was looking for wet cat food, not the dry kibble that I had put down for him late last night.

"Relax, Mochi. I will get you some fancy food."

He sang while I hunted for the ceramic bowl and cans of food. I labelled them with that exact detail so that I could locate it later quickly. Finding the goods, I cracked the can and dumped it into the bowl, setting it down on the floor out of the way.

The coffee maker was the first thing that I had unpacked last night, placing a single black mug beside it, for this morning. Locating a pod, that was the nightmare. I hunted through boxes and bags, tearing everything apart until I found a pod. It wasn't a good one, but it was one, and that was all I cared about.

I tucked things into cupboards where they belonged and found a box of crackers. Those would be perfect for a breakfast snack. Grabbing my coffee, I added a touch of cream and sugar, leaning against the counter and looking at the mess I created.

Taking a sip, I set it down on the countertop and dug into the large box on the table. Pulling out pots and pans, I started stuffing them in the cupboard across the room from the oven. Opening the oven drawer, I shoved all the cookie sheets and oven trays down there. Inside the oven, I stuffed two seasoned cast-iron pans. Snagging a few crackers from the box and taking a sip of coffee, I streamed music on my phone and danced around the kitchen while I put things away. I didn't even notice how much time had passed until my phone rang, cutting off the music I was dancing to.

Answering the phone, I put it on speaker so that I could finish the kitchen.

"Hey, afternoon. What's up?"

"I'm here, actually. I'm outside your door. I would have knocked, but my hands are full." Marco said, his voice stressing that I should hurry.

"Hold on, I'm coming to let you in."

Checking to make sure Mochi wasn't around, I went and opened the door. I took the baby bag and Wren in his car seat off Marco's left arm. Setting the bag on the living room table, I turned and caught Marco looking at my legs.

"Sorry, I lost track of time. I'm just going to grab some pants and I'll be back."

"Alright. Take your time."

Shaking off the feeling of his eyes on me, I pulled jeans on and headed to the kitchen. Marco had taken off his coat and placed it on the back of a chair, and he was holding his ribs. Dropping his hand when he saw me. He set the bags of food on the kitchen table.

"You got a lot done."

"Yes. I've been pretty busy. What about you?"

"Business as usual." He hummed.

"Sore ribs are regular business?" I questioned him.

"Sometimes, call it a workplace hazard." He laughed, but looked pained doing so.

"Want to let me have a look at those? I'm not a doctor, but I've seen broken ribs before and——-"

"Don't take this the wrong way, Ambrose, But I don't want to particular-ly—-"

"Eh, too bad. Lift your shirt and let me look." I said, ready to bring up how he choked me if he refused to do so.

He frowned, but slowly lifted his t-shirt. His ribs were an ugly purple and blue colour. His ribs looked pretty beat up.

"Yikes. I'd hate to see the other guy." I muttered.

"Gang members." Marco said flatly. Hissing when I placed my hands on his ribs.

"We have a bunch of gang members recently. Maddox had been shoving them out of his territory left, right and centre."

"We have as well. They are like cockroaches. Kill one and more return."

"I see. I think you should have these looked at. They might be broken."

"That matters little. I don't have the pleasure of taking time off to nurse broken ribs."

"Time or not, you should take it easy and—---"

Marco turned, and my fingertips trailed over his peck and I retracted my fingers, pausing only long enough to take in his figure. He was fit.

"What no abs?" I teased him.

"No, I don't fancy starving to achieve them." He said, pulling down his shirt.

"Hey, wait. I'm going to tape those, at the very least."

"I really don't need you to." He sighed and grabbed his side again.

"That, right there, tells me what your mouth doesn't, Marco." I said, crossing my arms at him.

He didn't respond to my comment, instead he went and picked up Wren out of the car seat.

"How old is he?" I asked, wondering since he was little, but not under six months, but I could be wrong, too. I wasn't an expert on babies.

"Eight months. Why do you ask?" Marco said, clearly bringing his guard up against me.

"I was just wondering. I thought he was over six months old, but I really wasn't sure."

"Yes. He is just eight months old this week."

"I see. Anyway, you really should let me tape your ribs up. I know how to do that."

"Ambrose, For the last time. I will pass. Please stop pushing it." There was an edge of annoyance in his voice, and I found it amusing, even though I shouldn't have.

"If I do, what will you do?" I said, more out of curiosity.

"That eager to find out what it's like when I'm mad." He said flatly, realizing what I was up to.

"Eh, perhaps. Sometimes I like to push my luck." I chuckled before walking up and taking Wren from his arms.

"Excuse you?" He said, shocked that I had robbed him.

"I wanted to see him. You see him all the time. I don't get to see little babies all the time. Besides, his weight can't feel good on your ribs."

Wren was wiggly in my arms today, a far cry from the last time I held him. But he was also giggly.

"Did you feed him sugar this morning, heavens? He is so wiggly."

"Romeao calls him worm." Marco sighed.

I snorted. Wren, Worm, close enough.

"Do you intend to teach him Italian?" I asked without thinking.

"Yes. He is Italian, through and through. If I don't, I am robbing him."

"Oh. Sticking heavily to the Italian blood, huh?"

"I want him to have the chance to be a made man in this family, if that's what he chooses. Romeao isn't like Maddox. Prominent positions are only given to those of Italian blood."

"Oh."

Looking at Wren as he wiggled in my arms, I spoke without thinking about it.

"I hope you give him the chance to make the choice if a life of crime and violence is what he wants." Realising what I said, I was quick to apologize. "Sorry, I shouldn't have said that. He's your child."

"You're fine. I will never make that choice for him, but I will teach him to be safe, given what I do for my job. I will protect that boy until my very last breath. Have no fear in that, Ambrose."

# 07 - Chapter Seven - Ambrose Grayson's Point Of View.

Three days into my job at the new ambulance bay, and both Mia and I were ready to call it quits. The people here were nuts. On our very first day, the first call was to attend a domestic dispute where the wife went bonkers and nearly murdered her husband with a frying pan. The second call was a robbery gone strange. The owner of the store locked the man in the ice bin.

I was thankful to have my very first day off. I was definitely going to rethink my choices about the career I was in. Mia dropped me back off at my apartment and crossed her arms.

"This looks unsavoury Ambrose, what did you get yourself into?"

"Relax, it's only temporary until I find something better."

"We will see about that." Mia said before she drove away, and I frowned. I knew she was only behaving in this manner because of the shitty day we had just put up with. There weren't as many Mafia related calls, but the calls that came through were worse than some of the worst mafia related ones we dealt with on the daily before here.

Inside the apartment, relaxed back on the couch, I closed my eyes and enjoyed the silence. Mochi curled up on the couch between my legs and I moved him before he could get comfortable.

"Sorry, old man, I have to get showered and changed before we can look at sleeping. You just go get in the bed, and I'll meet you there."

Peeling off layers of my work uniform, I was happy to see the shower. We used the showers at work, often. But Mia and I both turned those down, given we didn't know everyone in the new bay and did not trust anyone.

Washing in the shower quickly, I shivered when I got out. Part of me half expected to see Mochi there outside the door, pleading for his last chance to get more food before bed. Rather, I found him in the bed, waiting for me. Getting under the blankets, it didn't take long to pass out.

Waking up, the people above me were loud as fuck. Checking the clock, it was a little after eleven. Laying there until twelve, the noises were getting louder by the minute and I was growing annoyed. I understood they were working and shit, but I was far more respectful than they were being while they slept.

Grabbing my keys, wallet and phone, I messaged Mia, but she didn't answer me, so my next potential saviour was the man who helped me get here. Marco. I sent him a message telling him to leave the door unlocked and not to ask questions. He sent back an ok, and I shoved my phone back into my pocket. Leaving the apartment, I locked the door and bolted down the stairs. In my car, I breathed a sigh of relief. It was quiet.

Even with the heat on, I shivered all the way to Marco's in the tank top and sweatpants I was in. Parking my car beside his, I lightly closed the door and locked it, running to his front door, knocking once before running inside. I nearly slammed into him when I darted through the door. His arm stabilized me before he gave me a look, questioning everything.

"Are you alright?"

"Yes."

"I was heading to bed, I thought——-"

"Good, me too. I'll take your couch."

"Ambrose."

The way the man said my name had me pausing to look at him in the light from the kitchen. He was only in sweatpants and his ribs were taped, like I had forced him to accept from me days before.

"Long story, but I'm begging you to let me sleep on your couch, please, Marco."

"No."

"Eh! Please Marco——-"

"Hush. You can take my bed, and I'll take the bed in Wren's room."

"I couldn't ask you to do that, Marco."

"You didn't me too, and I'm not asking you to either. I'm telling you too."

"Oh."

Marco showed me to his room and waited until I got into the bed, before he shut the light off and closed the door. Laying in the bed, I didn't even have my phone. I left that on his table where I dropped my wallet and keys.

Marco came back just a few minutes after I pulled the blankets up to my chin. His phone flashlight was on.

"Sorry, I came to grab a shirt."

"How come?" I asked, trying to keep him in the room longer.

"The blanket in the space room in thin, I'm used to the thick one here—-"

"Then stay. You don't have to sleep in the other room. But is Wren warm in the other room?"

"Wren's room is warm."

"So the heavy blanket is more of a comfort thing, then?" I asked, not even sure why I needed to.

"You could say that." Marco whispered.

"Here, I'll scoot over and you can—--"

"You can stay on that side of the bed. I'll take the other side."

"But I'm clearly on your side of the bed where you sleep the most. This pillow smells like you." I muttered, before opening my eyes wide. "I didn't mean to say that, nor did I mean for that to sound the way it is, and I am sorry."

Marco laughed in the dark. I felt like an idiot.

"The scent is a custom scent. It's handmade for me."

I waited for Marco to mention that Ex-husband of his, but he didn't and I was too noisy for my own good. As he got into the bed, with a shirt on, I asked him.

"Did your ex-husband get that for you?"

He went nearly rigid before he relaxed again.

"His name is Theo, and no. He hated the scent."

"I don't understand why? It's a pleasant scent. You would know it any-where, if you even caught—--Oh." I finally understood.

"Yes, before you ask that, I cheated on Theo more times than I would like to admit to. And he knew he said it was the scent that confirmed my acts."

"I'm sorry, I shouldn't have asked." I said, feeling odd.

"You were curious, and I have had time to come to terms that I am to blame for my actions there. I knew what I was doing when I did."

"I think—--"

"Ambrose, we should sleep, it's already one."

"Oh right, sleep."

Marco and I both rolled away from each other and went to sleep. Sometime later, I felt him leave the bed, and then return. I rolled against him and touched my cold toes to his foot and he hissed.

"How the hell are your toes that cold?"

"Don't know."

"Remove them from the top of my foot."

"Make me Marco," I grunted, wrapped around the man purely for his heat. Trying to avoid his ribs, so I didn't hurt him.

"I will not play whatever game this is, Ambrose. It's four in the morning."

"Ugh, why." I whined.

He tried to roll away, and I went with him.

"Stop moving. I just want your heat, Marco." I chuckled.

"You're going to touch me with your chilly toes—-" Lifting my head from where I had tucked myself against Marco to steal his heat while avoiding putting too much of my body weight on him. I went to cut him off with my words, but after looking at him in the dark. I pressed my lips to his, pulling back only after realizing that I was the one who had just done that.

"Shit, I didn't mean to do that."

"Forget it."

I nodded, but did it again. Marco was a good-looking man. It wasn't like I hadn't been attracted to him. I knew it was a bad idea, but here I was for the third time, pressing my lips to his.

"Ambrose, We really shouldn't be doing this."

"Forget it happened in the morning." I muttered, letting my hands wander up his shirt, and he stopped my hand from going any further.

"Is this what you had planned when you decided you were coming to stay here?" He said, his tone accusatory.

"No, Not at all. They were loud, and I just wanted to sleep. You're a good-looking man, Marco. Trust me on that. But I didn't come here for sex."

"Then why the hell are you starting this?" He had a colder tone in his voice, and I didn't like it.

"My bad, Marco. You are attractive to me. I gave into a weakness." I hissed, trying to move away from him. Feeling slightly irritated, but not with the fact he denied me. I was grateful for that. But rather, he thought this had been my plan all along.

"I told you I wasn't playing your game, Ambrose."

"Let go of me then. I'm going home. This, here. What a mistake." I hissed, yanking myself out of Marco's grip. Getting out of the bed, he was right behind me all the way, right up to when in my shoes. I opened the door to the three feet of snow and blizzard.

"Looks like you're not actually going anywhere, Ambrose."

"Just my fucking luck."

"It is four in the morning, let's just go back to the bed and—--"

"I'm sleeping on the couch." I said, taking my shoes off again and heading towards the living room.

"Yeah, no. You're coming back to the bedroom with me and going back to sleep."

"Do you know what forcible confinement is, Marco?"

"Did you just threaten me, Ambrose?" His voice was dark, and I backed up slightly, feeling unsafe in that minute.

"Marco I don't—--"

He backed me into the door. It was cold on my back, and out of fear, I closed my eyes. I felt his fingers brush my cheek and his voice was low, and sent shivers down my spine.

"I'm a fucking mess, Ambrose. It's not a good idea to get involved with me."

# 08 - Chapter Eight - Ambrose Grayson's Point Of View.

W hen he backed up, it was like he had stroked my very soul and disabled the danger button that should have been screaming. But it was silent now, as I followed him back to the bedroom with only one thing on my mind. Putting my hands on this man in the deepest and sinful ways. I wanted to bend him to my liking.

In the bedroom, he stopped and turned to speak to me.

"Get in the bed and let go back to sleep."

"Sleeping in that bed with you right now is the last thing I have in mind." I said truthfully.

"Ambrose, please. Don't do this. I am not the person you want to get involved with."

"Says the man who refused to let me leave, and demanded I come back to the bedroom and to bed."

"I didn't mean this."

"Marco, you're giving me mixed signals."

"Ambrose."

The way his voice said my name was the last straw. He was pleading with me. It was in his voice, and I liked the sound of it. Marco had a few inches on me, but it didn't stop me from grabbing him by the chin and pressing my lips to his. Marco was breathless when I pulled away from him.

I sat on the end of the bed, my legs spread and forced Marco down on his knees and the shock on his face wasn't well hidden.

"Ambrose what are you——-"

"Quiet, you're alright."

"Ambrose, I've never been on the receiving end. If this is how you intend for things to play out. This might be too much for me." Marco said, the panic on his face heavy.

"I'll play by your rules Marco, I promise you this will be good. If it's too much, we can stop."

He looked conflicted, but he relaxed. "Fine."

"If you don't want to, we can just go back——-"

"I said, it was fine, Ambrose. I just didn't see this coming." He sighed.

"You are not the first to say that."

Sat between my legs in the dark, the moonlight peaking through the clouds, giving just enough light to see each other; I admired his body.

"I think you should remove some of this clothing, Marco."

He slowly reached for his shirt, and I spoke.

"Maybe this isn't a good idea with your ribs."

"I'm fine. My ribs are ok."

As if to double down on that idea, he moved like one would if they didn't have broken ribs that were only a few days old. Watching him flinch, I grabbed his chin, lightly and defiant eyes looked back at me, before he seemed to reel that emotion back in.

"Marco, don't push yourself if this is too much."

He stood up and yanked his sweatpants down, his boxers nearly going with them. It was hard not to touch him. I wanted to run my hand all over his exposed skin, but I took a deep breath, reeling in my lust. Marco was hard and tenting the front of his boxers.

"Do you have condoms and lube?" I asked softly.

"Yes, I do. I'll get them from the bathroom."

Marco disappeared into the dark and I pulled a hand through my hair, my heart racing with a childlike excitement. He returned just as quickly, placing the items into my hand. Setting the stuff on the bed, I made the come here motion with my finger, and he got closer, but he looked apprehensive.

"Don't look so panicked, Marco. This is in your hands. We stop when you want to."

He nodded, not saying a damn word. I didn't like that. Reaching out, I tucked two fingers into the waistband of his boxers and pulled him closer, before using both my hands to pull his boxers down.

"If you wanted them gone too, I would have taken them off."

"What fun is that? Unwrapping someone else's present."

Marco's breath hitched when I grabbed his cock and gave it a stroke.

"How long has it been since someone paid attention to you, Marco, and do be honest?"

"A year or more."

Spitting in my hand, I stroked him faster, and I watched his reaction to me touching him. I watched his stomach tense, and I let go of his cock and he groaned.

"Ambrose, why?"

"I don't want you to come yet. Just wait a little longer, then I'll let you get off."

His eyes held frustration, but he didn't show it. Pulling my shirt off, I tossed it into the dark. Marco stepped back, and I stood up, removing my own pants and leaving my boxers on. Proof of my arousal tenting the front of them.

"Come back here."

Marco stepped into my personal space again when I sat down on the edge of the bed once more and palmed his cock again. This time bring my head down to lick the bead of pre-cum off the tip. Marco shuttered, and I pulled back, worried his knees might buckle.

"Sit down."

"I should be alright, I just—"

"Marco. Sit. If you fall, then this is all over." I said flatly, and he did as I asked. I was amused that he was still listening to me this far. Lightly pushing him flat back against the bed, he flinched again, and I was ready to call it off.

"Wait, I'm fine, don't stop, please. Ambrose."

Watching him for a few minutes, I was satisfied that he was ok, and I was ok to continue. Moving his thighs apart, I placed my hand between his legs for leverage and moved, so I could lean down and take him into my mouth.

Marco cursed when hollowed my cheeks and worked on his neglected cock. His pubic hairs were dark like the hair on his head and trimmed short. Lifting my mouth off him, I stroked him again, though it was more of an afterthought.

I left kisses and bites on his flesh. I felt him jerk. Moving back down, I wrapped my lips around the head of his cock again and sucked him off.

"Ambrose, Wait——--Fuck."

His cum was warm and thick as it flowed into my mouth, and his saltiness engulfed my tastebuds. Pulling back, Marco sat up and grabbed my chin.

"Don't. That's not–" I swallowed his load, and he frowned. "-- I was going to say not to do just that."

"Too late."

"That's not pleasant, you don't have to——--"

"I don't have to do anything. I chose to swallow your cum, Marco."

The frown was still set on his face, but I spoke.

"Let me get you a drink and then we can have some more fun."

Returning with the glass of water from the kitchen, I handed it to Marco, and he drank a good majority of the glass, saving a mouthful.

"Here, rinse your mouth."

"Marco, I don't find your cum gross or disgusting, but I'll accept the water, regardless."

"Do you want me to help you with that, Ambrose?"

"No, What I want is you to find a comfortable position on your stomach with this—" I smacked his ass. "Up for me."

It took him a few minutes, but he did as I asked, and I found the lube pouring a generous amount into my hand.

"This is going to be a little cold, and probably uncomfortable, but please try to relax."

Massaging the lube into his hole, I was able to slip a finger in after a few minutes, and then another one.

"I feel bad for every male I've ever just fucked without lube." He hissed.

"It's not always this bad."

"I fucking hope not."

I felt bad, but pressed on because he had not indicated to stop. Three fingers deep was really pushing it with Marco. He was clearly trying his hardest not to call mercy on this one. He relaxed when I found his prostate and applied soft pressure to it.

"Marco, Does that feel good?"

"I have no idea what you're doing, but it feels nicer than before."

"I'm massaging your prostate."

"Gross."

I chucked and slowly removed my fingers, and he spoke.

"Wait, why did you stop?"

"I've loosened you up. I'm going to gently enter you."

Marco looked unimpressed, but let out a deep breath and tried to relax. While he did all that, I added more lube to his hole. Yanked my boxers off, and put the condom on, and lubed it up.

"Just relax, ok? It's going to be a little uncomfortable at first."

Pressing my cock tip into him, he hissed and tensed. Using my free hand, I rubbed his back. My cock slid in slowly and he grunted.

"Please tell me you're almost in."

"More or less."

"Brush up on the meaning of gently, next time."

"Your tense, that's why it hurts Marco."

He remained quiet even as I got all the way inside him, and stilled. I waited until I felt him relax around me before I asked him if it was still uncomfortable.

"Not nearly as bad as before."

"Good, I'm glad. I'm going to move slowly. If it's too much, let me know."

Aiming for his prostate with each thrust, Marco slowly became less and less bitchy about the pain, and more and more vocal. Grunts and various other sounds came out of him. He came again with no stimulation from my hands or his. Marco kept clamping down on my cock and it was hard to stay hard and not blow my load in him.

"Marco, simmer down on that. It's hell on my cock. I'm trying to make this pleasurable for you and you're milking my cock for what it's worth." I hissed. I felt my orgasim building, and I gripped his hips roughly and slammed into him.

I grunted when I came and pulled out once the aftershocks of my orgasm ended. Marco moved on the bed and took the condom off me. Before I could tell him I was fine to clean it up, he wrapped his mouth around my sensitive cock and I hissed, yanking him off with his short hair.

"Sorry. Too much, fuck."

"Let me get a cloth for us both."

The sun was coming up, and Marco shook his head.

"Hurry, we need to sleep."

I wiped my cock and then cleaned Marco, who seemed less amused with my gesture. Neither of us bothered with clothing. We just crawled into the bed and aimed for sleep.

When I woke up a few hours later, Marco was gone, and I realized it was real. Not all dreams. Marco and I had sex. I could hear someone moving around and I figured it was Marco. Pulling all my clothes back on, I made my way out of the bedroom and towards the kitchen.

It wasn't Marco, though, but rather his boss and Wren in the kitchen. Taking a few steps to go back to the room, he spoke.

"Marco isn't home. He had to do something for me, but do come join us for breakfast."

I got the feeling breakfast wasn't voluntary, and I took a deep breath and headed into the kitchen.

# 09 - Chapter Nine - Ambrose Grayson's Point Of View.

-------------------------------------------------------

Sitting at the table, I got the feeling that Romeao wasn't exactly a fan of mine. He was polite, but almost to the point of it being unnatural and had to digest. Silently praying, I hoped Marco would come back sooner than later. Accepting the cup of coffee from him, I couldn't help but feel he was trying to scare me away from Marco.

"Thanks for the coffee, I'm going to head————"

"Stay right where you are, Ambrose. I have breakfast nearly made, and we should have a conversation."

His words were still polite, but they had a bite to them now. I debated texting Marco for help, but even if I did, I wasn't sure he could actually help me here. This was his boss, not the other way around.

He set a plate of bacon and eggs in front of me and gave Wren some eggs. Before he sat down with his own cup of coffee and breakfast.

"Please, eat. I'm sure your body could use the energy after what you did to Marco."

Coughing on the coffee that had been in my mouth and throat when he hit me with that comment, I took another sip to ease the discomfort.

"I have no idea what you're talking about." I said, politely.

"I'm sure you know exactly what it is I'm talking about. But that's not the point here."

"I'm pretty sure I'm figuring out the point here." I said dryly.

"Marco has had it pretty rough, with Theo, his ex-husband, and the abuse he committed. I'm sure I don't need to continue with this."

"If you're trying to scare me off of Marco, I'm not going to play into this." I said, eating the food through the bits of conversation.

"Oh, You're the least of my concerns Ambrose. If I wanted to scare you off, breakfast wouldn't be how I would do so. But this is a gentle warning. I have put much work into getting Marco to where he is right now. I will not have you, or anyone else, jeopardize his healing."

The food and coffee were sitting like lead in my stomach now.

"I don't think you need to throw veiled threats at me. We hardly know each other. But I can promise you, Marco doesn't need you to protect him. He knows what's wrong and right."

"Marco has his sweet Wren to worry about. You're an afterthought that he doesn't need."

Finishing up the coffee, I took my empty breakfast plates to the sink and turned around after grabbing my phone, wallet, and keys.

"Thank you for breakfast. I'm sure you'll find a way to explain this to Marco."

I ruffled Wren's messy hair before leaving. Truthfully, I was fuming and wanted to go back in there and threaten Romeao, but that was unwise. Even I knew that. I passed by Marco in his SUV when I was just leaving his house in my car. The roads were nearly clean and my car had been cleaned off too, probably by Marco. He called moments later, and I ignored his call. It was wrong to do so, but I didn't want to cause problems with Romeao for him.

Heading home, I was thankful that the building still let me in and it was quiet again. Tossing my stuff on the countertop, Marco had texted and called a few more times since the call in the car. His last text said just to call him. I had no clue what Romeao was going to tell him, but whatever it was, it had not gone over well by the stream of texts. I felt like the biggest of douchebags, after taking what I had from him and not speaking to him, but Romeao's comments got under my skin, and I couldn't promise my intentions and acts benefited him.

Laying back in my bed, Mochi mewed at me, touching his paw to my cheek. Under my blankets, Marco's cologne was able to be picked up by my nose on my clothing, and it was irritating. But at the same time, I didn't want to shower.

Tucked under my blankets, I tossed and turned, finally upsetting Mochi, and he left me in bed alone. Grabbing a pillow, I tucked it under my arm and head, and forced my eyes to close. My phone rang on the nightstand, but I ignored it. Telling myself that sleeping was more important. Once it went silent, I relaxed into the bed again, not realizing how tense I had been.

A few hours later, I dragged myself out of the bed. Changing my clothing, I brought the tank top up to my nose, Marco's spicy scent, still on the fabric even after sleeping in my bed. Grabbing my phone, there were more calls and texts from Marco, and the texts increased in length and curse words, no doubt as he got madder about me ignoring him.

Tossing my phone on the couch when I left the bedroom, I sighed. Mochi danced around my feet for food, and I accepted his song and fed him. It was two in the afternoon when I checked the clock.

My phone went off again, this time, though it was my dad's ringtone. Heading to the couch, I retrieved my phone, and he spoke.

"Afternoon. Are you still coming for dinner? Your mother is home and would like to see you."

"Afternoon. I'll be over shortly, I just need to shower and get dressed, you know, look presentable for family dinner, so that she doesn't think I'm incapable of looking after myself."

"You ok? You sound exhausted."

"Long night, and strange morning, and I just woke up from a nap."

"Right, you must have the day off, then?"

"Yes, absolutely. I miss my ambulance bay, and my boss. This place sucks and the crimes here are worse than at home. I would ask you to demand we come home back to our base, but honestly, it's not worth it." I groaned.

"I wouldn't, anyway. It's still safer there and I'm sure it's not as bad as you say."

"I'll see you in an hour or so."

"Alright, drive safe. It's a little snowy out there." Dad said, laughing before he hung up the phone. Setting my phone on the arm of the couch, I walked back to my bedroom and dug through the closest until I found some decent jeans and a sweater. After dealing with Romeao, I wasn't really in a mood to care about what other people wanted.

Getting dressed, and brushing my teeth, I looked at myself in the mirror and hated the face that looked back at me. I looked exhausted. Turning the taps on, I washed my face and felt a little better. Feeling that this was good enough of an effort, I washed my hands and located everything I needed before leaving the apartment.

Thirty minutes in the car, I got to Dad's and seeing mom's car in the driveway too made me anxious and I really didn't understand why. I hadn't seen her in a few weeks, and I missed her, but knowing she was here stressed me out for some reason.

Heading inside, I could hear my mother telling my dad all about her trip and all the things she did. It sounded like she had a great time. Hanging up my keys and setting my wallet on the hall table, I took my shoes off and walked into the living room.

Mom stopped talking and made a comment under her breath before speaking to me.

"Nice to see you've come for dinner, Ambrose. Next time possibly sleep before you come, those dark circles are going to age you more than anything else."

"Thanks, nice to see you too." I sighed.

Dad gave me a sympathetic look before he spoke.

"You look as exhausted as you sounded on the phone, and you said you slept? Where?"

"I did, for hours, but I had a long night and I hope not to repeat that."

"What did you do after work yesterday?" Mom asked, her arms crossed.

"Went home, tried to sleep, went and hung out with a friend, slept like shit."

"Is that so?" Her eyes narrowed on me.

"What?"

"You were up to some funky shit, Ambrose Grayson. Don't you lie to——-"

"He is an adult, his personal life is his now." My dad said, trying to get her off my case.

"Don't you start that with me. That boy has no personal life. He's up to some shady shit. My woman's intuition tells me so." My mother hissed, pointing her slipper at me.

"Mom, put that back on your foot. We don't need that kind of chaos."

"I didn't come to this country for you to start acting up and getting into shady——-"

"Elena, go easy on the boy, he just got here——-"

"Hope, for once she's right, dad."

"Huh?"

"I was definitely up to some shady shit."

"I highly doubt——-"

My phone rang and Marco's name flashed across the screen and Dad went visually stiff.

"Are you going to answer that?" My mother said,

"No, he's not." My dad said sharply.

"I'm not."

"Why the hell does he have your number, Ambrose?"

"Better question here. You know his boss, Romeao? Is he an enormous threat?"

"What the hell did you do, Ambrose Grayson?"

"Oh boy, that's a loaded question."

Spilling all my sins from the night before, minus some details, Dad was mad.

"You slept with the man who just a few weeks ago tried to choke the life out of you? Did I get that right?"

"Yeah."

My mother was far from amused. She just stopped even speaking to me in English. She was mad that I had slept with Marco after he choked me.

"Of all the men you can choose, you pick him."

"I didn't pick him, per se. We slept together once. And Romeao basically threatened me. Now Marco is mad because, as you see, I'm ignoring him."

"Romeao is normally balanced. It's Marco. That's who you need to watch for in that family. He is the one Romeao uses to solve all of his issues. But if Romeao has threatened you, over Marco, be ever so careful if you intended to pay that hand, Ambrose. I know Romeao, but I can't help you if piss off that bull."

# 10 - Chapter Ten - Ambrose Grayson's Point Of View.

R egret weighed on me for two weeks. That was how long I had been ignoring Marco, and not by my choice. He stopped sending me messages after the first week and I figured he was just beyond pissed off at me. I wanted to tell him what Romeao said, and how it bothered me, but it wasn't like he was wrong and that's where I struggled. Marco had Wren to worry about, and I was just an afterthought, but having it thrown in my face, that I didn't like.

My work schedule was all over the place too. I went from working days to working nights, and that almost seemed like a blessing. The people that lived around me seemed nice to me.

Marco's SUV was in the parking lot when I arrived. Last night was a long shift, and I just wanted to shower and sleep. I had the weekend off and I was thankful for that. My last patient of the night had been a next to dead gang member who died from his gunshot wounds in the back of the ambulance while I fought to keep him stabilized. I needed the weekend just to feel better.

I could hear Marco screaming from the front door of the apartment building. A few of the henchmen hung out in the lobby area away from him, and I didn't blame them.

"Watch it. Marco's in a foul mood." One henchman said.

"Oh yeah, I hear him."

"It was a dreadful night."

"I know a bit about that."

"Yeah, I would imagine so."

"Thanks for the heads up"

Heading up the stairs, I crept to my door, sliding the key into the lock. The hairs on the back of my neck stood up.

"Ambrose."

"Marco—-"

"Oh, we have much to talk about."

I didn't even have a chance to ask if he wanted to come in, finished unlocking the door, opened it and took the key out. Shoving me inside the apartment, he closed the door behind him and flipped the lock again.

"You have a lot of nerve avoiding me." He said, his voice cold, like the first time in the alley.

I let out a yawn as I kicked my boots off and went to feed the Mochi.

"Avoiding you implies I know where and what you're up to, which I don't. It was more like ignoring your calls and texts." I sighed.

"Like that's any better."

"It is when I enjoy living."

"What—-Romeao? He said something."

I didn't confirm that. I just went about my nightly tasks before I got ready for bed. Marco blocked the hallway so I couldn't head to my bedroom.

"We need to talk about—--"

"There isn't anything for us to talk about." I said, ducking under his arm.

He grabbed me and pinned me against the wall. His forearm against my throat.

"Ambrose, I'm not playing anymore. I'm pissed. Did he or did he not say something to you?"

"Move your fucking arm, Marco."

His eyes dared me to make him. Using the back of my hand, I tapped his ribs, and he hissed and moved back from me.

"Sorry, you really should get those looked at." I muttered.

Marco was holding his ribs, and he was clearly trying to keep his anger at bay from my actions. Marco took out his phone and called someone, putting it on speaker.

"Marco, what do you need?"

Romeao's voice stirred a bitter feeling in me.

"Did you tell Ambrose to stay away from me, Romeao?"

"Yes, I won't lie to you. There is enough to worry about. You don't need to wreck the progress you have been making, but to clarify my answer for you and parties. You need someone who will commit to helping you grow. If that isn't what can be offered, then it's pointless."

"Romeao, you can't make that choice for me." Marco said sternly.

"I'll admit, my words were harsher than they should have been towards Ambrose. But after the Theo disaster, I don't need you losing everything we have both put into getting you where we are, and I won't allow anyone to ruin that. That being said, I didn't tell him in exact words to stay away from you. I did, however, tell him he was an afterthought you didn't need."

"How is that even remotely appropriate?"

Yawning, I flicked off the kitchen light and spoke, interrupting Marco's and Romeao's conversation.

"Go home Marco."

"Excuse us, Romeao, watch Wren for me. I need to deal with something." He said, clicking the red phone button.

"I told you to—-"

"I heard you, and I don't care. I'm not listening to you."

"Stay, go, I don't care. I'm going to bed. I've had enough regret and murder for two weeks."

"You regret what happened?" Marco said bitterly.

"No. I regret not telling Romeao to piss off when I had the chance."

"Do you think that is wise?"

"Does it look like I care?" I yawned.

"Ambrose, I'm not leaving until you tell me what I can do to make this rift better."

"Rift? Marco, we slept together once, we aren't—--fuck sake." I hissed, grabbing him by the jacket. Tired and annoyed.

"What are you doing?"

"We are going to bed. We can argue about this shit later. Wren is looked after, yes?"

"Yes, Romeao will watch him."

"Good."

I shoved his jacket off his shoulders and tossed it and all the contents on the floor. I worked on undoing his belt buckle too, and then the button.

"You're undressing me pretty quickly, but you haven't told me what you want from me." Marco said lowly.

"I did. We were going to sleep, I said. I don't want to fight the jeans for your heat." I muttered.

"I see."

He kicked his boots off, and then his pants, and his shirt, too. He yanked my sweater and shirt off all together and shoved my pants down my legs. When he was done, the only thing left was my boxers.

"I'm going to yell at you in the morning."

"Are you?" He asked.

"Yes. Be prepared."

"Alright."

Laying in the bed beside him, I curled against him, and enjoyed the feeling of his heat. Even as it helped lull me to sleep. His heartbeat was comforting. I wouldn't actually yell at him in the morning. I had no reason to.

Opening my eyes later, Marco was still sleeping. I tucked against his side. Last night's events playing over in my head again.

"Stupid man." I hissed.

He looked far too peaceful sleeping that way. So I pressed myself closer to him and ran my fingertips across his hips. My guilt at ignoring him after taking what I did made me feel bad. But I deserved it.

"This isn't the yelling you promised me." Marco said, his voice full of sleep.

I trailed my fingers around his flesh and noted every reaction I got from him. Before I spoke again.

"I'm sorry. I shouldn't have ignored you. I was thinking only about myself and how I was feeling."

"It's fine. I get it."

"No, you don't, Marco. I took something from you that night, and we shared something. And I was a douchebag and ignored you all because he hurt my pride and feelings."

"He told you that you were an afterthought I didn't need. I think I, too, would be hurt."

"It still doesn't excuse my behaviour and for that, I am sorry, Marco."

"I can understand your reasoning, but what I can't understand is why you couldn't be honest with me about what he said, not even once. You just had to send a text."

"I wanted to know if he was dangerous before I made any choices, and according to my dad, it's not him I need to worry about. It's you. You're the one who does his dangerous, dirty work."

"Yes, Romeao does use me for the dirty work."

"He said you're dangerous."

"Yes, Ambrose, I am."

"I don't see it."

"But you have before. Don't forget that."

"I don't actively think about the fact you tried to remove my head from my shoulders."

"You should. I told you I'm a mess, and Romeao just further proves this."

"Romeao proves nothing, other than that he thinks I'll ruin your progress in healing, which let me be clear. I do not have that intention, nor did I when I made the choice to sleep with you."

"That pisses me off. He had no right."

"He wants to protect you and your son. I can understand why."

"He overstepped. He is my boss, but he is not in complete control over my life. We have been friends for a long time, and I get his concerns are well placed, but I won't have it, and the words he said to you were unacceptable. Even for him. I would like to say that if the gangs hadn't stolen and attacked us, he might have been kinder to that morning. But I would make excuses for him, and I can't say he would have been nicer."

"I know a little about your gang troubles. They bleed into my job, too."

"Yes, I can imagine they do."

"Our last call early this morning before I came home and bumped into you, and all your yelling was a gang member, taken out by one of yours, probably. He was just barely hanging onto life, and I did everything in my power to keep him alive, but he died in the back."

"Yes. We are shooting to kill them now. We do try to keep outsiders from being involved. He must have made it back to a populated area, and that's unacceptable. You shouldn't be dealing with them." Marco said darkly.

"You're going to yell at someone about this, aren't you?"

"Yes. I will. But not right now. Truthfully, I am enjoying your heat as well."

"I'm sorry again."

"You've already said that."

"Then let me prove it."

"By all means, if that is what you feel you must do."

Trying to get out of the bed, he held me against him.

"What are you doing?"

"Trying to prove that I'm sorry."

"How?"

"Going to your house, and telling him to piss off."

"Oh no, we are not about to do——-"

"Not we, me." I corrected him, feeling somewhat better and sure that I would feel much better after I told Romeao off.

"Ambrose, that is not a wise idea at all."

"I only wanted to chat over breakfast." I said, smiling tightly.

# 11 - Eleven - Ambrose Grayson's Point Of View.

----------------------------------------------------------------

**M**arco clarified he didn't want me to instigate a fight between Romeao and I. So even as we pulled into his driveway an hour later, he repeated himself about not causing a fight.

"For the third time, Marco, I understand."

"Do you, because you have this look, and I would call it a scheming one, but I'm not positive that's what it is?"

"You have next to nothing to worry about. I know how to behave."

While he was in the room, at least. Marco let me into the house in front of him and gave me a look. Romeao came out from the kitchen and they spoke in Italian. whatever he was saying too, was making Marco heated. Without thinking about it twice, I touched Marco's hand. That seemed to reel back some of his anger with Romeao.

"Wren's in the kitchen. I just finished preparing lunch. Help yourself." Romeao said politely, and I got the hint. He wanted me to get lost.

Looking Marco up and down and seeing he was calm again, I said I would behave, so I went to the kitchen. I didn't like it though, I would have much rather stayed and told Romeao what I thought about his comments.

Wren was giggling in the high chair, playing with a set of plastic keys. Romeao had food set aside on a plate for him, clearly cooling off. I sat in the chair closest to Wren and watched him play. This kid did things to my heart. He was adorable.

Marco and Romeao returned, and things looked good between them for the moment. Marco grabbed plates for us all and Romeao filled them with a pasta mix.

"Would you like to sit with Wren?" I asked, going to stand up.

"No, you're alright where you are." Marce replied.

Romeao gave Wren his food when we all sat down to eat. Wren didn't eat it, though. He was just playing with his food, and it was alright until he shoved the pasta off the side of the tray onto the floor. Romeao didn't pay him any attention, rather he ignored him and continued his conversation with Marco.

Putting a noodle on the end of my fork, I blew on it before holding it out for Wren to take. He put the noodle in his mouth and made quick work of it.

"Guess he wasn't into plain pasta." Marco said, standing up and coming to clean up the pasta on the floor.

Passing Wren another sauce covered noodle, he took it and held onto it for a few moments before he put it in his mouth and chewed.

"I'll get him some covered noodles. You eat yours." Romeao said, standing up.

"We are fine, thank you." I said politely, though there was some bite to it.

Marco looked at me, and I smiled back softly.

"I see you're still not over my comment." Romeao said, as he sat back down.

"Glad you're aware." I gave Wren another noodle and ate a few bites while I waited for Wren to want another noodle.

"We both only want what's best for Marco." He said, before taking a bite of pasta.

"Best for Marco, or best for your best interests, Romeao?"

"Marco's best interests are mine."

"If you say so."

"Ambrose—-"

"No, It's alright Marco. Ambrose is free to express his thoughts and feelings, regardless if we agree or not."

"You tried to push me away from Marco. You had no right to do so."

Wren screamed at me, and I passed him another noodle. Marco looked uncomfortable at the end of the table.

"Yes, I did. But as for rights, his behaviour comes back to me, Ambrose. I'm sure you can understand that Marco is a pivotal player in my family."

"Pivotal player or not, mafia boss or not, let me tell you in the nicest and politest way I know how. Keep your option out of my relationship with your underboss. It might not end well for both of us, but get involved like you did before, and the veiled threat you gave me at breakfast a few weeks ago won't even be my starting point."

"Ambrose, I asked you to—--"

"Quiet Marco." Romeao said, softly. His eyes locked with mine and his words were surprisingly gentle given I threatened him.

"I will do my best to let you figure things out with Marco then, but only because you have the guts to threaten me. I could make you disappear, Ambrose Grayson, don't threaten me again because you got away with it this time."

My appetite was gone. Marco and Romeao finished their meals in silence, and I fed as much of mine as I could to Wren, who accepted the offering.

As soon as Romeao left after putting Wren down for a nap, the sound of the door clicking closed, Marco crossed his arms and sighed.

"Whatever posturing you were doing with Romeao is bad. That is the behaviour that will get you killed Ambrose. Surely you don't act that way with Maddox. What the hell are you thinking?"

"You think I interact with Maddox?"

"Do you not?"

"Occasionally, but never more than a few words. And as my father said, it's not Romeao I have to watch out for, it's his underboss, and I'm pretty sure I know how to stop that." I muttered.

"You got under his skin, Ambrose, and that takes a lot. You are aware he carries a weapon on him, yes?"

"I figured."

"Never again, understood."

"Arguing with him? Or threatening him?"

"Threatening him, Ambrose. Fuck."

"I survived, so relax."

"Relax? Thank god, you're an EMT. You can administer medical attention when you give me a bloody stroke."

"Paramedic, actually, there is a difference in schooling and activities the job requires. But yes, I can administer medical attention to you."

Marco cursed at me in Italian, and I snorted. Even annoyed and mad at me, Marco was still attractive.

"I take it your Ex-husband had no issues with Romeao."

"Issues, no. They were close."

"Right, so someone already stacked the playing field against me."

"I don't believe it's anything like that. If it was, I doubt he would have backed off."

"He didn't at first."

"The air in there was tense and uncomfortable. I would much prefer if you don't do that again, for both your safety and my sanity. Even though you threatened him, he wasn't that upset about it. He made a comment to me in Italian before he left."

"Did he?"

"Yes, he said he was glad to have someone who would put me in my place." Marco said, pulling a hand through his dark hair, and narrowing his eyes on me. "Is that what you intend to do, Ambrose? Put me in my place?"

"When I know what place best suits you, perhaps I will." I chuckled, stepping into his personal space, and giving the man a gentle hug.

"What are you doing?"

"Self soothing, with your body."

He wrapped his arms around me.

"Were you even scared that he might harm you?"

"Yes, truthfully, yes, I was."

Marco sighed.

"I have a few hours before I have to handle some things for Romeao. He will most likely be back to handle Wren, but regardless, stay here, wait for me to get back."

"I can watch Wren tonight. I have the weekend off. I don't work again until Monday night, but I will have to head home in the morning to feed my cat."

"I will take you tomorrow to feed the cat, then I implore you to come back for the night again."

"Where was this behaviour when I was trying to find a place?" I said, snorting, meaning it as a joke.

"If they bother you too much, let me know. I can deal with it." Marco said, suddenly.

"No, thank you. When you deal with things, you yell and they hide in the lobby." I chuckled.

"Last night wasn't a good night for either of us."

"Working nights isn't all bad. I've slowly been getting used to it, but you're right, last night wasn't a good one."

"Working nights are clearly taking a toll on you, Ambrose."

"That was only last night. Some nights, I still have energy."

"Good to know."

"As I said, I can watch Wren."

"He sleeps most of the night, so it's mostly just being here in case he wakes up. You're welcome to use the guest bed."

"Is he allergic to anything?"

"No."

"Good, are you?"

"No, not that I know of."

I nodded and stepped back out of Marco's arms. The scent of his cologne leaving my nose.

"Enough self soothing?"

"Yes, my tank is full again."

"Good. Let me go check on Wren."

I sat on the couch in the living room, and Marco came back with a grumpy-looking baby. He wailed when Marco set him on the floor. Marco didn't even seem fazed, he just let Wren scream his feelings out.

"Did you wake him?"

"No, he was awake."

"He looks miserable."

"Can confirm that. He bit me when I grabbed him out of the crib."

"What?" I said laughing.

"He grabbed my hand and bit it."

"He's got your attitude."

"I fucking hope not." Marco hissed.

"At least he's cute."

Wren was still upset. He butt scooted all the way to the couch and stuck his hands up. Marco gave him a soother, but did not pick him up.

"He can have some floor time, much to his dislike."

He pulled out the soother, dropping it and screamed. Marco was clearly breaking with each scream that Wren was making, but I broke first and picked grumpy up off the floor. Marco retrieved his soother and wiped it off before giving it back to him. He was quiet now, and inched closer to Marco, until he was lying on Marco's chest.

"He always wants to be glued to me when he is miserable."

"Of course he does. You're his father, and you comfort him."

"He comforts me, too." Marco said softly, rubbing Wren's tiny back. Within a few minutes, he was back to sleep and his little hand was bunched in Marco's t-shirt.

# 12 - Twelve - Ambrose Grayson's Point Of View.

Marco woke Wren up an hour later, and he was two times more miserable than he had been. Marco fought with him to eat dinner, bathe him and get him to bed. When Romeao showed up, he alerted Marco they were doing something together tonight and I would be on my own with the baby. I was more than ok with being left alone with the baby.

Marco left me with the TV remote and free rein of his space. I was glad I had thought ahead and fed Mochi extra food. Sitting on the couch, the baby monitor was quiet. Getting up, I went to check on Wren despite the silence.

Marco had only been gone for an hour, and Wren was sitting up in his crib, just silently touching things in his crib. He looked up at me and I watched his bottom lip tremble and I sighed.

"Your dad is going to kill me, Wren, but let's go."

I picked him up out of the crib and tucked him to my side, and grabbed the soother in the crib, too. I offered him the soother, and he took it. He was probably teething, and that was why he was miserable.

Touching his forehead, he was a little warm, nothing to be super worried about. I tried to set him on the floor in the living room so I could see if there was something Marco had for teething, but Wren had other ideas. He grabbed my pant leg and cried.

"Ok, Ok. I won't put you down. Poor peanut," I rubbed his back, "I'm sure daddy has something for you."

After hunting up and down, Marco had nothing for Wren and he got fussier by the minute. I checked his diaper, and it was clean. Marco was busy with work, and I didn't want to bother him. Picking up my phone, I dialled my dad, hoping he was still up and moving at this late hour.

"Ambrose, it's late, are you ok?"

"I'm ok, but I need a favour. Are you busy? I can figure something else out if you are?"

"I'm just getting out of a meeting with a couple of guys. What do you need?"

"Could you swing by the pharmacy and pick me up some infant medication and a teething ring, please?"

"Ambrose, I would ask you where you are, and whose baby you have, but I don't even think I want to know."

"Yeah, It's best if you don't know."

"Are you at his house?"

"Yes, I am. I can give you the address if you need it."

"That would be helpful. I'll video call you when I get to the store and you can pick the things you need."

"Thank you! I can't leave and get something. Marco is working and I don't have his car seat, and I don't want to worry Marco, if he comes back and Wren and I aren't here."

"I don't mind, at least helping with Marco's child. Marco, that is a different story, Ambrose."

"Dad, please—--"

"Marco is dangerous and you know it. How long before he puts his hands on you again like he did his ex-husband?"

"Dad, I will not discuss this with you. I get you think Marco is dangerous and I will admit, he is. But that is not the guy he shows me. Believe me when I say I will not allow Marco and I whatever this is, to get to the point of violence. He doesn't need that, and neither does his little boy."

"The only thing I can do is believe that, Ambrose."

"Are you driving?"

"Yes."

"Why didn't you hang up? You know better than anyone about how dangerous it is to talk on the phone and drive? Do I need to remind you how I have found some people—---"

"You're through the car speakers. Relax."

"Good. Good."

"I'll call you back once I'm in the baby aisle."

"Ok."

Dad hung up, and I tucked my phone back into my pocket and took Wren with me as I walked to the kitchen. With my attention fully on him now,

I could see the rash on his cheek. He was chewing on his soother the best he could, dribbling all over us both.

"What a mess," I cooed and yanked my ringing phone out of my pocket. "Oh, it's my dad. We best answer him."

Hitting the answer button, the aisle of baby things came into view.

"Christ, he looks just like Marco."

"He is Marco's son. What did you expect?" I laughed, and Wren just chewed away on his soother.

"I knew it was his son, but did he need a carbon copy?"

"I think his carbon copy is cute." I said, snorting.

"Ok, Ok. Back to why I called. What do you need?"

"Infant medication for teething, and a teething ring, and a couple bibs for sure."

After finding all the things I wanted, which also included some outfits that he really didn't need, I found them way too cute to leave there. I sent dad some money once we got off the phone.

I walked around the kitchen bouncing Wren. He settled back down on my shoulder to sleep and I was worried if I stopped he might wake back up and be miserable again. I let dad in when showed up. I would explain to Marco when he come back home why my dad was here and apologize for giving out his address.

"Oh look at him, poor kid."

"Thank you, you're a lifesaver."

"I'll send you back the money I didn't use."

"No, no. Keep it for coming and bringing me all this stuff."

"You know, I saw Marco tonight, with Romeao. We all met tonight. The three families."

"Romeao said they were working together tonight. Hence, why I have the baby?"

"That kid could use some outside interaction, you know, outside the Mafia. It's good you're here. Despite that, I don't like the idea of Marco and you."

"I can't say if we will end up that way, but I think if we do, it wouldn't be the worst thing. I'm not fond of the mafia, but I could live with it if I had to."

"You turned out to be a good kid, Ambrose. No matter what your mother says, she and I are beyond proud of you."

"Thanks, but don't get all sappy on me. You need to get home before it gets any later."

Dad left, and I went to put the stuff away, a sleeping Wren with me the whole time. I was grateful to see that dad had picked up a few different kinds of medications and a couple of the teething rings. I popped the teething rings into the freezer and left all the medications on the counter for Marco. I left all the clothes in the bag on the table and took Wren to the living room.

I laid him on the floor and he started to get fussy, so I laid down beside him. He had his head on my arm up near my shoulder and he went back to sleep pretty quickly.

Once I was sure he was asleep, I got up, moving him slightly off my arm and turned all the lights off before grabbing a pillow and coming back to lie with him on the floor.

When he fussed again at three am, I changed his diaper while he screamed and redressed him after, taking him to the couch and letting him lay on my chest and rubbing his back.

Marco came home around four am, and Wren and I were still laying on the couch and I heard him click his tongue before coming into the living room. He bent down to take Wren, and I slapped his hand away gently.

"Touch the baby and I will murder you, Marco. This is the longest he has slept."

"Long night?" He whispered.

"I had my dad pick up some things for him. He is teething and very miserable. There's a few teething rings in the freezer, a few different types of medication on the counter. I didn't give him anything because you weren't here, and I didn't want to give him medication without your consent, as his parent. There are some outfits and bibs in the bag on the table."

"I got the alert when your dad pulled into the driveway. I wasn't too worried. I figured you asked him to come, since I know he doesn't have my address, and if he needed something, he could have asked when I saw him a few hours ago."

"Yes, he told me about the meeting with the three families. Did that go well?"

"About as well as it could."

"Good, bad?"

"It went well for a few minutes. Maddox wants Romeao and I to offer him assistance with the docks and a few shipments, and that would be fine, but Alessio, you've met him, at the complex, he's the don of the third family, and his underboss is one of two partners of my ex-husband. He makes working hard together. I get it, I do. But he doesn't make things any easier for me."

"Yikes, you're in quite the pickle, aren't you?"

"You could say that for sure."

"I have faith in you."

Marco sat down on the floor in front of the couch, with his back towards me, and laid his head back against me. He said nothing, but I understood the words he didn't say.

He was tired and stressed out. He wanted comfort and I could give him that.

"It means more to me than you could understand." He whispered.

# 13 - Thirteen - Ambrose Grayson's Point Of View.

M arco took the baby back to his crib, and he was unhappy about it, but Marco returned to the living room not too long after.

"There, he's back to sleep in his bed, where he can get some more sleep."

"What if he wakes up?" I spotted the baby monitor in his hand. "I see. That makes sense."

"Yeah. Let's go. We both can use a few hours of sleep, too."

"If I go to sleep now, I'll mess up my sleep-ah, forget, I can use the rest." I said, following behind him, all the way back to his bedroom.

He wasted no times getting undressed, and I spotted a few new scraps on him.

"How did you get these?"

"Oh, I trained some newer guys after the meeting. I caught my side on one prop of a fence we use for training."

"Your ribs are still broken?" I questioned him.

"Yes. They are."

I crossed my arms in the light from just his closest as he was tossing his clothing into the hamper there.

"Then what in the holy shit are you doing? Are you trying to puncture your lung or---"

"Shh, Relax, I was ok. Romeao knows I'm still injured and tried to talk me out of training them, but if they are too work under me, I want them trained properly. Or else what can I do with useless henchmen?"

"You could get injured further," I said, frowning at him. "Please, just take it easy, if you need to do training."

"Of course, I always am."

I pulled off my top and sweatpants, crawling into Marco's bed.

"Not going to object to sleeping in my bed this time?" Marco teased, crawling under the covers beside me.

Scooting closer to him, I ran my fingertips along his chest and leaned down by his ear. "Hardly, I've been inside you, Marco."

"Not so off limits now that you've fucked me, huh?" Marco said, as he turned off his closest lights with an app on his phone.

"Your bed and room are a personal space. I don't enjoy taking over other people's personal spaces. If I can help it."

"I've invited you into my personal spaces"

"Yes, in more ways than one." I muttered, and he sighed.

"You pervert."

"You said it, not I."

"You thought it, though, and you know it."

"I might have." I laughed softly into the dark of the room. My hands, still tracing parts of Marco's skin. Drifting my fingers around on his skin, I dipped my fingers lower on his stomach and I felt him draw in a breath. His muscles tensed under my fingertips.

"Just what are you up to, Ambrose?" He whispered, his accent mildly wrapping into his words.

"Trying to convince myself we should be sleeping." I hissed, moving my fingers up from his lower stomach.

He wrapped his arm around me and pulled me tight against him. He had me squished right up against him now, and I couldn't help myself. I licked his flesh. That was right in front of me.

"Ambrose."

"Sorry. I couldn't resist."

"Go to sleep. We need too, we only have a few hours before the Romeao is going to show up. I don't know how long after that I'll be allowed to lounge in bed. He might have work for me."

"Right, ok." I tried to roll away, but he wouldn't let me. Pressed up against his warm skin, I settled down and closed my eyes. His breathing and the sound of his heart beating were oddly relaxing and helped me fall asleep.

I woke up when I felt the bed move. Cracking open an eye, Marco was trying to slip back into the bed.

"Sorry, I didn't mean to wake you. You looked like you were having a good sleep."

"Mm, I was." I muttered, closing my eyes again, before rolling on my back and stretching out completely. "What time is it?"

"Ten am, Romeao got here at seven. He let himself in and kept Wren amused, and fed him breakfast while we slept."

"Oh shit, wow. Is he still here?"

"No, he went home once I got up, and oddly, he gave me the day off."

"Hmm. Where's Wren?"

"Sleeping again last night took a lot out of him. He needed a nap."

"I feel that. Come here." I groaned, trying to pull Marco closer to me, now that he was back in the bed. His cologne was the first thing I picked up on when I laid my head on his t-shirt..

"Everything you own is this scent."

"Yes."

"You smell delightful."

I closed my eyes again for a moment. Marco ran his fingers along my exposed flesh, under the blankets. When he tucked a single finger under the band of my boxers along my hip. I opened my eyes. "What are you doing?"

"Oh, so you are still with me?"

"Hardly." I hissed.

"That's an understatement." He laughed lightly as he cupped my cock. "Something else of yours is hard."

"Ugh, why. Don't get me going this early."

"This isn't early anymore, Ambrose, and you were so eager to touch me last night. It's only fair if I show you the same attention."

"That was last"-His fingers dipped into my boxers and he grabbed my cock- "Night. Fuck"

"It was only a few hours ago," Marco said, his voice practically talking me out of my pants.

"Let me pee, and when I come back, I'm going to put my hands all over you."

"I sure hope that's a promise."

I rolled out of the bed and hurried to the bathroom. Relieving myself, I darted back to the bed. About to jump on Marco, but stopping at the last minute. Remembering his broken ribs.

"Were you about to jump on me, Ambrose?"

"Yes, actually."

"How old are you?"

"Old enough to know that if I jumped on you, I might break more of your old man bones." I snickered.

"Come here. I'll show you broke old man bones." He hissed. Crawling back in the bed, under the covers, I looked at Marco.

"What?"

"Cold hand." I said, before sticking my hand under the band of his boxers against his warm skin. He hissed and yanked my hand out from under his boxers. Clearly not amused with my action.

"I'd say sorry, but I'm not, and honesty is more important." I laughed.

"Yes. I agree."

Marco got this look in his eyes and rolled us over. He hovered over me, and I laughed

"This won't work in your favour, Marco. All you've done is give me access to your cock."

To further my statement, I reached down and cupped his cock.

"If I fall on you--"

"My hands make you that weak, do they?" I said, teasing him.

I rubbed my hand over his cock a few times, and I watched his arms tense.

"Perhaps we should find a much more comfortable position for you, Marco."

"Are you teasing me, Ambrose?"

"I might have been at first, but now, I just want to make you tremble under my fingertips." I said, removing my hand from cupping his cock, and he lowered himself back to the mattress beside me.

Reaching over, I slipped my fingers under his boxer band and took hold of him.

"Ambrose."

"Hush. I want to help you relieve some of your pent up stress, and a massage is such a good way."

"What are you getting out of this?" He said, looking conflicted.

"Satisfaction. Knowing that I helped you relax, among other things." I whispered, leaning over to kiss him. "You should lose these boxers. Give me the range to explore your figure."

Marco slipped his boxers off when I removed my hand out of his way. He settled back down into the bed, and I touched his stomach, trailing my fingers down his torso, down to his cock. I wrapped my hand around his cock and stroked him. Marco wasn't hung like a horse, but he was thick. I was almost jealous of his thickness. Marco was circumcised.

"Ambrose, slow down, or this isn't going to last very long for either of us." Marco pleaded with me.

I slowed my pace down to crawl, and Marco gave me a look.

"Too slow and torturous now?" I asked, before pepper kisses on his skin.

"That's just mean." He grunted.

I picked up the pace again, and just as I felt his muscles tighten, I took my hand off him.

"No, this is mean."

Marco threw his arm over his face. Lifting the blanket, I shoved it down, and that got his attention. He moved his arm and watched me as I opened his legs and got between them.

"Ambrose, you don't need to-"

"Enough, let me treat you."

I took him into my mouth and he threw his arm back over his face and muttered something in Italian that I didn't understand. Moving back off of him, I spoke.

"Look at me Marco."

He moved his arm and cast his eyes downward, lifting his head slightly.

"You will be the death of me." He muttered, as I took him back into my mouth and set to make the man come undone.

I pulled back off Marco, stroking him at a faster but even pace and he hissed. Ropes of his cum hit me before I could fully understand why he was tensing up. I clicked my tongue and Marco looked at me, while his cum was dripping down my face.

"My bad."

# 14 - Fourteen - Ambrose Grayson's Point Of View.

After my weekend with Marco, going back to work felt like shit. But here I was, walking into the ambulance bay with Mia, discussing our weekend. We still really didn't fit in here, but the night crews that worked with us were a little more chatty than normal. They asked about our weekends and brought up the last call. They seemed pretty curious about what had gone on. Mia just sighed.

"Our last call on Friday coded and died. Probable gang violence."

"Shit eh?" Someone said,

"Yeah. Seems pretty common." I muttered.

"It definitely is becoming more common here. It never used to be as bad, but with the mafia—-" His partner elbowed him in the ribs and he shut his mouth.

"We are no stranger to the mafia. We are from Lake Haven." Mia said, shrugging. The alarm sounded and Mia and I loaded up into the ambulance and headed to the call. It was a standard call, not mafia or gang related.

Mia and I loaded the patient into the back of the ambulance. I ran through the basics.

"Tell dispatch to alert the hospital. We have a heart attack patient coming in, complaining of chest pain and shortness of breath." I said.

The ride was brief, and we took the patient inside the ER and passed him off. The doctors and nurses took him off our hands. We collected our things and headed back out to the ambulance.

"Do you ever just tire of this, Ambrose?"

"Of saving lives?" I asked.

"No, of the mafia, it seems like every guy or person in this city and ours is mafia related one way or another. I went for a coffee on the weekend and chatted up a really nice-looking guy, who didn't look mafia, you know. No pressed suits, just dressed down and fine as hell. But he was definitely mafia too, I knew after just being around him."

"I get it. Seems like they are everywhere, but I don't think they are all bad, and there has to be someone who isn't Mafia related."

"I swear it's just you and I anymore, Ambrose." She said,

I pictured Marco and felt a little guilty.

"Yeah, haha. It seems like it's just us, anymore."

There was no way right now that I was going to open my mouth to her about Marco. Not when she thought we were the only ones left without personal Mafia ties.

"But hey, If you ever get a Mafia boyfriend, Mia, I hear they get paid pretty nice." I said, laughing.

"One of these times, I might just say fuck it and try it."

"Oh, yeah?"

"Yeah, They seem nicer than normal men, and like you said, they get paid well. Just once I would like to sleep in, not just on the weekends, you know."

"Oh, trust me, I get it. I spent the weekend with Marco—-"

"Who's Marco? His name sounds Italian—Wait. Ambrose, are you dating a mafia guy?" She asked, about filling her face.

"We aren't dating."

"But you didn't deny he wasn't Mafia, Ambrose is he—-"

"Nope, we aren't discussing him."

We got another call. After responding, she turned back to me.

"We are not done with this conversation. I need to know more about the Mafia man you're seeing, since you are even more picky about men and you don't even like the mafia. You've never looked at a man a second longer if he states he's mafia, and you're staying at this man's house."

"It's not as big of a deal as you're making it." I muttered.

The entire drive to the call, she didn't stop talking. I got it, though. She wanted to know what was so different about Marco that I let my guard down when he was part of the Mafia. And not just a grunt, but an under-boss. But she didn't need to know that part.

Grabbing the bag and dropping it on the stretcher, Mia and I wheeled the stretcher up to the door, a woman opening the door for us.

"Oh, thank god you're here, he's in here."

She showed us to a dining room, where a man was sitting on the chair, a fork sticking straight up in his hand. Mia gave a look, and I looked back at her.

"We're going to need to get the police involved here." I whispered to her.

"Hmm. Agreed." she whispered back.

Looking back at the lady, I spoke, as I set the bag on the table.

"Alright, hi there. Can you tell me how this happened? And a bit about yourself. Are you on any kind of medication? Even regular over-the-counter ones?" I asked him, and he looked terrified, and I wondered if it was because of her.

I leaned down by his ear as Mia spoke to her and I spoke softly, "Blink twice if she did this and you need us to get you out of here."

The man blinked twice, and I spoke.

"Mia, he's going to shock. We need to get him loaded up and to the hospital as quickly as possible."

The women looked at him and looked at us.

"I'll get his meds. Can I ride in the back with him?"

Before I could tell her no, she was gone and Mia looked at me and the man, helping me load him up on the stretcher after prepping his hand for transport. She appeared again, a bag of medication and her jacket and purse. She walked out to the ambulance with us and when she tried to climb in after him; I spoke.

"Unfortunately, ma'am, you will have to meet us at the hospital. We don't allow people to accompany patients in the back, as there isn't enough room to accompany more than the patient and the attending paramedic. We encourage you to meet us at the local hospital, however."

She looked pissed, but shoved his meds in my hands and stomped off back inside. I closed the door, and Mia got in and we drove off. The man finally spoke.

"God, thank you. You're a bloody life saver, that women is fucking nuts."

"Is she related to you?"

"She's my wife! But she's completely lost it. She stabbed me with a fucking fork."

Mia called dispatch to have a pair of officers sent to the hospital and be waiting for the old lady to show up.

"She's definitely something." I muttered.

"The police are going to be there right! They are going to protect me from her!"

"They are being notified, yes, and they will handle the rest." I said softly, checking the packing around the wound just before we pulled into the hospital. Getting out, Mia and I wheeled him inside, two uniformed cops waiting for us. They got him checked in, and Mia and I were just waiting for our stretcher back. We could hear the old women in the hallway fighting with the cops.

Getting our stretcher back, we were leaving. The old woman spotted us and Mia and I watched as she stabbed one cop with another fork.

"Holy shit, this town is fucked up."

"You're telling me." I muttered, shoving the stretcher faster down the halls, not wanting to be any closer to that old woman.

Heading back to the bay, we cleaned up the stretcher and relaxed while we waited for another call to come in. My phone rang, and I didn't check it the first time, but by the second call, back to back, I fished it out of my pocket and answered it.

"Hey Marco, what up? It must be——-"

"Are you working?"

"Yeah, I am. What's up?" I asked, Mia's full attention to me now.

"Fuck. Just my motherfucking luck." He snapped.

"Marco, what do you need?" I asked.

"I had a run in with a knife, and I might need a hand."

"Where are you? Can someone around you call emergency services?"

"I'll try. Hold on."

The line went dead, and I looked at Mia.

"Get the medical bag, now. We are about to get a call."

Two minutes later, the bell rang, and Mia took the call, not even giving the others a chance to intercept it. Inside the ambulance, we raced towards downtown and cops had arrived in the area. I spotted Sasha getting out of a cop car as we stopped, and he spotted me. He pointed to the alley of a building, and Mia and I raced that way once we got the stretcher out of the back to get to Marco.

Marco was leaned up against a wall, his hand covering his wound. He was dressed in normal clothing and had a bag beside him. Grabbing the medical bag, I set to work, and Marco hissed.

"You took your sweet time."

"What the hell happened and do you have a weapon on you?" I asked.

"No, I was getting shit for the baby, and it was fucking gang members. Fuck." He snarled. I grabbed gauze and moved his hand once I had mine covered with gloves. Pressing the gauze to the wound, he howled and Sasha finally got into the alley.

"Are you armed?" He asked.

"No. If I had been, Ambrose would be playing CPR on a corpse, not this shit." He snapped, clearly in pain.

Getting Marco onto the stretcher, he was very unhappy with me, more so when I applied pressure to his wound.

Mia barely said two words the whole time. It wasn't until Marco was out of my hands and we were waiting for our stretcher that she said something.

"Ambrose, seriously, that man doesn't seem safe. He—--"

"Don't." I hissed, not feeling like I could handle this from her right now.

"Ambrose, he is clearly an influential player in the Mafia here. What the hell are you—-"

"Lower your voice. You are being way too loud about this. As far as either of us is concerned, we don't know a damn thing."

"Ambrose, you're trying to protect him!" She snapped.

"Wrong. I'm protecting you."

"From who! What the hell did you get yourself into?"

"Look, I'll tell you when we aren't here, ok. But just trust me, what we just did, it didn't happen. That's just how the game is played."

"Oh god, Ambrose, he is a big player. Isn't he?"

Before I could answer her, I spotted Romeao, and he spotted me. He also spotted Mia. She spotted him and his fancy suit, and she gave me a look. She knew he was also part of the Mafia.

He stopped and spoke.

"Thank you for tending to him, both of you."

"Please keep me updated, I beg—-" He cut me off.

"Of course. Once I know something, I'll be in contact."

He was barely a few feet away, and she spoke, something in her voice I had never heard before, fear.

"Ambrose, you fucked up. I don't know what position he holds, but that was definitely his boss."

"Marco is an underboss." I whispered, watching her eyes widen. "We can have a full conversation about this another time. Right now is not the time."

Truthfully, I didn't want to talk about Marco until I knew he was going to be just fine.

# 15 - Fifteen - Ambrose Grayson's Point Of View.

As soon as I was done with work, I went back to the hospital. I needed to see Marco. With my own eyes. Romeao had let me know with a text that he was alright, but it wasn't enough. At the nurses' station, I asked for Marco. The nurse looked at me strangely, but I was pretty sure that was because I was still in uniform.

"What relation are you to the patient, Mr Di Salvo?"

"I'm his partner. We are together." I said, lying through my teeth, knowing this was the only way they were going to let me into the room.

"Right, take this badge and he's up on the second floor."

I clipped the badge on my shirt and headed up. I was mildly regretting not changing out of my work pants and jacket. Getting out of the elevator on the second floor, I asked for Marco at the desk and pointed to a room just down the hall. Heading down the hall, I stopped in front of the door and knocked on the door softly before popping it open.

It was a private room, not surprising though. I figured he would have that at the very least. Marco was up. Romeao was here with him, too. Wren was nowhere to be seen.

"Sorry, I'm not intruding, am I?"

"No, come in, close the door." Marco said.

"I wanted to make sure you were alright."

"I told you he was alright." Romeao said, politely.

"I know, I got your message, but I needed to see with my own eyes, after how he was the last time I saw him."

"That's completely understandable. I told Marco to expect you. He told me you might be in after you sleep, but based on your uniform, sleep isn't something you've done." Romeao said, looking at Marco.

"Pardon me for asking, but where is the baby?"

"He's at Marco's with a henchman. He is perfectly safe there."

I frowned. Romeao really must have trusted this person to leave Wren with him.

"If you're so worried about Wren, by all means, go to Marco's and check on him."

"Sleep while you're there, too. Please." Marco said, his eyes locked on mine.

"How long do you have to stay in the hospital?" I asked, changing the subject.

"Five to seven days, and they checked out my ribs while I was here, too. They aren't too concerned with the ribs. They told me how lucky I was that vital organs were missed, but that I'm looking at upwards of six months of full recovery."

"Three, and you will be back at work. You won't sit idle that long, even if I demanded it." Romeao sighed.

"What will you do without Marco in the field?" I asked.

"Those under Marco will pick up the slack, and I will handle Marco's work."

"I can watch Wren. I really don't mind." I said.

"Then please, bring me your schedule for work, and we can work—--"

"Ambrose has a job and a life—--"

"Hush Marco, I don't mind helping."

"Then stay at my house, so you don't have to commute back and forth, and you can care for your cat. Bring him too."

"I would hate for him to wreak something or—-"

"I don't care, don't fight me on this. Just do as I've asked. You can get proper sleep. Somewhere I know you're safe, and Wren will have you while I can't be there, and Romeao can't all the time."

"Fine." I groaned, realising that Marco would not give up on this matter, even in his condition.

I stayed with Marco a little while longer, before he sent me away when I started yawning. Heading home, I sent Romeao a text, letting him know I was going to rest before taking myself and my things to Marco's. We exchanged numbers to keep in contact with Marco.

Crawling into bed after I showered, the apartment was quiet. When I closed my eyes, Marco's pained face popped into my head. I inhaled and exhaled repeatedly until the thoughts about Marco that way disappeared and sleep flooded in.

Mochi didn't let me sleep very long. Just three hours later, according to the time on my phone, he was standing on me, kneading my back over and over until I got up. He wanted a snack. I understood that.

"Let's go. I know you're waiting for your morning snack."

In the kitchen, I poured him some food, and he screamed about it, until I set the dish down.

"If you need anything else, you can find me back in bed for another hour."

Laying face down in the bed, I passed out again pretty quickly. I heard nothing more until my alarm went off at two p.m. Mochi was going to be pretty salty about the car ride, but he was going to love all the extra space and things he could get into at Marco's. I was still really worried about him wrecking something of Marco's or hurting Wren.

Mochi had never even seen a baby before. This was going to be an unfamiliar experience for him. I was just praying they got along.

Packing up Mochi and a ton of other things, I got them into my vehicle, after a few trips, and locked up. Marco's car was in his driveway now, having been returned, probably by Romeao. I was pretty excited to see Wren.

I knocked on the door, and a man opened it.

"Your Ambrose right?"

"Yes, that's me."

"Good, good. Romeao said you would be over shortly. I have some things to take Marco at the hospital."

"Then please, don't let me keep you."

"Wren is in the living room in the playpen, laying down. He was miserable this afternoon."

"Alright, thanks for the heads up."

The man left, and Wren didn't wake up until after I got all my things inside and took mochi to Marco's room. I let him out and closed the door, setting up the litter box I bought along the way. That way, it was new and clean for a few days.

Wren cried from the playpen, and I washed my hands before going and picking him up. I checked his diaper, and it was still clean, so I walked around with him for a bit before taking him to the kitchen and finding something I knew he could eat. I watched him eat away until he wasn't eating anymore. I warmed him a bottle and took him back to the living room and set him in the playpen. He cried when I did this.

"Oh pumpkin, shhh. I just need to check on your bottle, then I will be back and I can hold you."

With the bottle in hand, I returned to the living room and plucked him from the playpen and held him as I fed him with the bottle. His eyes drifted closed as he drank from the bottle. Carefully, with him in my arms, I set him back down in the playpen after he was done with the bottle and I hovered until I was sure he would not wake back up and start screaming again.

I let Mochi out of Marco's bedroom, and he looked around, heading to the kitchen. He stopped under the highchair and cleaned up the few bits of food that Wren dropped. When he was done with his stolen snack, he went around sniffing things. That all stopped when he found Wren. He got as close as he could to the side of the playpen and watched him. I played with a dry patch on my skin absentmindedly as I watched Mochi. I was worried that he might hurt Wren.

He sat down and let out a meow.

"Leave that baby alone, Mochi."

I turned my back to make sure that I left nothing dirty in the kitchen and when I came back, Mochi was in the playpen with Wren. He wasn't bothering Wren. He was laying down in the corner, minding his own business, his eyes closed.

Deciding not to move him, I checked my watch and groaned; I had a few hours before I had to go back to work, but Romeao said he would have someone cover that for me. I still felt bad that I couldn't take more work off Romeao's shoulders. That way, Marco didn't feel so guilty about missing so much work.

Relaxing back on the couch, I watched Wren sleeping. My phone vibrated in my pocket. Pulling it out, Marco was calling. Pressing the answer button, Marco's face popped up, and he smiled.

"I see you're lounging on my couch." He chuckled.

"Yes, it's a comfortable couch, but I can also watch Wren while he sleeps in the playpen." I whispered.

"Can I see him?" Marco said. I could only imagine that he missed his son.

"Sure, hold on, I can bring him to see you in a little while, too."

"Would you?"

"Of course."

I flicked the camera around and even in the dark, Marco had hawk eyes.

"Is that your cat?"

"Haha, yeah. I tried to keep him from—-"

"I'm not worried. Well, maybe for your cat. Wren is going to smother him." Marco said, laughing.

"I was worried about Mochi hurting Wren, but he has made no attempts. He's hurt no one before, and I'm hoping he won't try with Wren. I would feel terrible."

"If you think Mochi was it, is safe in there, and won't hurt Wren, I trust your judgement. But if it happens, we can go from there."

I nodded, realizing he could see me nod. I flipped the camera back around.

"How are you feeling?"

"Eh, I feel like I'm sitting here doing nothing when I could hunt down the asshole who did this and make an example out of him."

"Are the cops involved?"

"Yes, Sasha and another man were here earlier to take pictures and ask a bunch of questions."

"Lukas, His name is Lukas Black. He is the Maddox's underboss, Andrei Mihail's partner."

"How do you know so much, for someone who keeps so far away from all this?"

"I still listen. I just don't get involved. Plus, I know some partners of Mafia members pretty well. Sasha and I really weren't good friends until after his accident. We talked, but Ryer, his partner, really helped open him up to more than just his work husband, Lukas."

"I think you would know plenty, Your job and who your father is. It must be hard to keep away from the Mafia."

"Yeah, you're not wrong."

"Once I'm out of here, I'll help you find somewhere else to live and I'll find——-"

"Marco, I don't want you to push me away." I muttered.

"What?"

"I don't want you to push me away. Despite it all, I enjoy spending time with you and Wren, and Romeo ain't so bad."

"Are you saying that you don't dislike all Mafia men? Is that what I actually hear you saying, Ambrose?"

"There are a few mafia men that I don't see as all bad, and you make that list. So count yourself lucky, Marco Di Salvo."

# 16 - Sixteen - Ambrose Grayson's Point Of View.

Getting out at the hospital with Wren, I was positive I had driven no one's car safer than I did in Marco's car with Wren in the backseat. Wren didn't want to be in the car seat for a second longer than he had to. Pulling him out, I carried him on my hip inside and collected a badge at the front desk. I still had to work in a few hours, but I didn't mind taking Wren to see Marco. I wanted to see him, too.

Not even stopping at the desk, I opened Marcos' door, and there was a doctor inside, frowning, as he checked Marcos' wound.

"Hope I'm not interrupting."

"No, no, please come in. I was just checking Marco's wound. I'm Doctor Dominic McLaughlin." His bright red hair pinned up in a bun on the back of his head was definitely telling, right along with his light Irish accent that lingered.

Using the hand that wasn't holding Wren, I shook his hand when he wasn't touching Marco's wound and removed his gloves.

"How's Marco's stab wound?" I asked.

"I would ask if you would like to see it, but most people wouldn't."

"I've already seen enough of Marco's blood and guts for a lifetime."

"Were you present when this all went down, Mr?"

"Ambrose Grayson, And no, but I was the paramedic that tended to him all the way here."

"Oh, I see. That must have been a tough call."

Wren screamed, trying to get his dad's attention. And the doctor excused himself, and Marco groaned. "Give me my baby. I want... no need to hold him."

"Of course, here" I passed Wren off to Marco, who took him, and was clearly uncomfortable, but said nothing about it.

"The nurses asked about you today, or rather, they asked if my partner was coming to visit again, or if I wanted to call you. I didn't understand who they were talking about at first. I figured my ex-husband. But no. Turns out, it was you."

My face heated, and I spoke. "I can explain—-"

"No need. But you should know the nurses talk about you."

"Huh? Why?" I asked, confused.

"They think you're handsome and polite, and something about you being strong because of your job." Marco said, winking at me.

I sighed. "You would think they had better things to do than gossip. They have you to look after. You're pretty easy on the eyes too, Marco Di Salvo."

"Do you have to work tonight?" Marco asked.

"Unfortunately, yes, but I'm looking to take a few days off just to make things easier. Or knock down some of my hours." I said.

"When I'm out, we can't look for something more acceptable for you, apartment wise."

"Oh? Who said I was going to let you have your house back?" I laughed, saying it only as a joke.

"Paying rent in childcare?" Marco asked, his eyebrow raised.

"Maybe." I shrugged.

Wren was just cuddling against Marco, not moving very much.

"Is he sleeping?"

"No, he's just enjoying my company." Marco said, looking down at Wren. "I missed him."

"He missed you too, Marco."

"Couple more days and I should be able to come home, this place and all this, it's driving me nuts, and I don't think I can handle another few days more of tasteless hospital food."

"It's not that bad. You just need some salt and pepper." I said.

"No, you need hopes and vivid dreams to make that shit better." Marco groaned before looking at me. "I'm probably going to need help when I get out, and I don't want to ask too much of you."

"No worries. I'll help you where I can. Besides, Wren and you are the only friends I have here."

"Oh. Really?"

"Yeah, besides Mia, but she's been busy with other things lately. Nights are killing her, and I get it."

"How are you handling the nights?"

"Fine, I worked a lot of long nights when I first started. Mia and I worked days for the last couple of years, though, so it's a pretty large transition for her. Not so much for me. I picked up extra shifts with other partners looking for extra hours, too."

"Sounds like you're well adjusted to this life, life of a paramedic." Marco said.

"Kind of like how you are well adjusted to your job." I said, softly smiling at him.

"Romeao is glad that it was you and your partner that tended to me."

"I'm sure he was."

"I was too. If I died, at least I was in good company."

My mouth went dry, and it took a few minutes to regain enough moisture in my mouth to speak. "I was prepared to do anything I had to in order to keep you alive in the back of my ambulance."

"You are very dedicated to your position."

"I try to be."

"Can I see your hand?"

"Sure?" I said, sticking my hand out. He took it into his own and held onto it tightly.

"I'm glad we met, though. I wish it was under better circumstances."

"Please, you're hardly the first person to attempt to murder me while I'm responding to a call."

Marco frowned.

"Nothing serious, yet, haha." I said, laughing it off, trying to get the frown off Marco's face.

"You must have seen a lot of things?"

"Unfortunately, yes, but it's the DOAs (dead on arrival) that really stick with you."

"Like your gang member?"

"Yes, like the gang member, but I doubt he will be the last to be loaded into my ambulance."

"He will if I have my way. You shouldn't be put in the way of danger from my job." Marco said, looking down at Wren. "If something happens to me, and I don't get to come home from my work, I want you to take Wren."

"Marco, I—-"

"No, Please, listen."

"Alright."

"I want him to have a normal life. That way, he gets to have a choice in his own future."

"What about your ex-husband, could you not—-"

"No, absolutely not. I would never allow that. Theo is never getting my child. He is too far into that life too. As are his partners. You, you are not."

My chest was tight, and I didn't like him talking like this. I understood why he was, but I hated it.

"Please, can we speak about something else?" I asked.

"Yes, but—-"

"Another time we can speak about this subject, but I can't right now. I still have your fucking blood on my other uniform and I can't do it." I hissed, yanking my hand out of his and rubbing the uncomfortable spot in my chest.

"I'm sorry. I should have allowed more time to pass before bringing this up. I didn't even think how this would affect you. Ambrose, I'm sorry."

I checked my watch and spoke.

"Is Romeao coming soon?"

"Yes, he is coming in a few minutes, I'm assuming."

"I have to leave, I'll take Wren—-"

"No, you can leave him, and I'll have Romeao take him home."

"What about his car seat?"

"Romeao has one too."

"Alright."

I stood up, and Marco grabbed my hand. Causing emotions to well up inside of me in such a strange way.

"Excuse me for this." I said, before leaning down and pressing my lips to his.

"You're excused." He said when we parted. His pupils dilated, his lips parted as he licked them. I reached out and ran my fingers through his hair before looking at Wren once more.

"I'll come back and visit when I'm done with my shift."

"Come back after you've had time to rest."

"Maybe, we shall see." I laughed, leaving just as Romeao was coming up the hall. He said hello, and I greeted him back before returning the badge down at the front desk and heading back to Marco's. I had to get ready for work.

Stripping down in his bathroom, I flicked his shower on and looked in the mirror. Tired eyes looked back at me and I sighed. Seeing Marco like that was enough for me to realize he was right. There was a possibility he might not come home. But then that was the same for my dad. There was always a possibility he, too, might not come home.

I was catching feelings for Marco and his son and I was all too aware of it happening, but I wasn't trying to stop it either. I was letting it happen.

Under the spray of the shower, I used Marco's body wash, and it was comforting. I scrubbed away at my skin until I was positive that I had scrubbed away some of my stress and maybe a layer or two of skin.

I got dressed in my spare uniform when I got out and dried off, snatching some of Marco's cologne, mostly because I liked the smell and it reminded me of him. Walking to the kitchen, I made a cup of coffee with Marco's coffee maker and a couple of pieces of toast.

Chewing on my toast, I checked my emails and texted my dad to check on him, and be nosey about Marco's stabbing. I fed Mochi and told him to behave and stay out of trouble, more so when Romeao came back here tonight with the baby. I didn't need Romeao to not like my cat, when he was just starting to like me.

Grabbing my keys, wallet, phone and jacket, I left Marco's.

Arriving at work, Mia was waiting for me with a coffee in her hand.

"Ugh, you're such a lifesaver."

"I know, I know." She said, before pausing and taking a deep breath.

"You smell like the mobster, Ambrose."

I shrugged, and she sighed.

"You smell expensive, and I oddly remember the scent in our ambulance. Marco right, his name was Marco."

"Yes, his name is Marco."

"Look, I won't get into your business, but is he at least nice?"

"Yeah, he is to me, and his son is cute, too."

"I have a mafia member next door to me in my apartment, and he asked me to dinner, but I didn't want to tell you. But at least now that I see you aren't immune to them, I don't feel bad that we went out together for dinner." Mia said.

"You went for dinner with a mafia member?"

"Yes, but that is not important. You are involved with a high-ranking mafia member, Ambrose. Are you sure that's something you want to do?" She asked. She really did not know how involved Marco and I had actually been.

"I'm just allowing this to go wherever it will. I'm not going to stop it, but I'm not going to force it, either."

"You owe me a conversation about Marco, Ambrose, then I'll tell you about my neighbour Max." She said, wiggling her eyebrows. It was like her entire view on the mafia had changed, and I wondered how this guy had managed it over one dinner, the other night she was ready to rip me apart about Marco and how dangerous he was, now she seemed just nosey about him.

# 17 - Seventeen - Ambrose Grayson's Point Of View.

-----

At the end of our shift, we pulled back into the bay, and I spoke.

"Mia, I'm sorry for the other night at the hospital—--"

"Nah, I get it. You like him and you wanted to protect him. Honestly, I went home and mulled over the idea a ton and I got it. I would have done the same thing and I've never known you to be a terrible judge of characters, so if you think he's good enough of a guy to be with, I won't question it, or his job."

"Seriously?"

"Yeah, I don't see any reason to."

"Hm. What are your plans?"

"Max and I are having breakfast this morning, and then I'm heading home to sleep. You?"

"I'm heading to see Marco at the hospital. I'm going to get in my truck, get a coffee, change out of my uniform, and then head up."

"Have fun with your expensive boyfriend." She laughed, heading out.

Getting into my truck, I stopped and grabbed a coffee, and drove to Marcos. Romeao's car wasn't there. I assumed he might have been at the hospital. Getting changed quickly, I grabbed one of Marco's jackets because I didn't have my own, other than my paramedic one, and I didn't want to wear that in the hospital. I was off the clock.

Badge clipped onto my shirt. I headed up and didn't bother to knock. I just headed into the room. Romeao, Marco and Sasha, and my dad looked at me.

"Huh. This is... awkward." I muttered.

"My coat suits you." Marco said, smiling, trying to break the silence in the room. Wren was sleeping tucked in beside him.

"Should I step out? I don't want to interrupt."

"No, you're welcome to stay. You obviously came for a purpose." My dad said, in uniform, looking at Romeao.

"Please, come. I'll move if you want to sit by Marco." Romeao said, getting ready to stand up.

"No need, he can sit on the end of the bed." Marco said.

Sasha, who was standing beside me, spoke.

"You smell like Marco, his cologne... Oh."

"It's his jacket." I muttered.

"Yeah. It's not. It's too heavy—-"

"Detective Doornail, that is my father. Zip it." I hissed.

"Ambrose, I sure hope you're using acceptable words." My dad said, glancing at Romeao, as if he was reminding who we were in the presence of.

"Come sit." Marco said, his hand patting the bed. Biting my tongue, I made my way over and sat down. Marco chuckled.

"Sasha's right. You smell like me. Used a couple sprays, huh?"

"Eh, maybe."

My dad cleared his throat, getting our attention.

"I apprised Maddox of the situation, and Sasha is doing some digging into the situation. We are going to call this a freak incident. I trust you two families can work something out and sort this. The gang violence is getting out of hand."

"We intend to handle this quickly and quietly." Romeao said, glancing at Marco.

"Ambrose." My dad said.

"Yeah?"

"Dinner at the house this weekend. I expect you, and you're plus two."

"My plus two? Oh!" He meant Marco and Wren.

"We will be there." Marco said, meeting eyes with my dad, and I turned to look at Marco.

"You can't, you need to rest and——-"

"I will be fine. I can go home tomorrow afternoon. So, I should be able to go for dinner with you, like he has asked."

"No. I won't allow it, you're injured and I won't——-"

"Ambrose, you are a long way from a position of demanding or refusing to allow me to do something."

"Surely Romeao won't allow this. You need to heal." I looked at Romeao and he looked at me, his words polite.

"If Marco feels this is something he needs to do, then why should I stop him?"

I looked at Sasha, the only one in the room who seemed to understand what I was going through.

"Ambrose, get used to this. If what I think is happening here is, then this is an everyday battle with their type. You won't win this. That isn't a wall you can't move." Sasha sighed while he checked his phone.

I wanted to grind my teeth in annoyance, but I didn't. I just crossed my arms and exhaled loudly. "If you hurt yourself, on whatever mission this is to prove yourself to my father, or whatever. It is solely your fault and your problem, and if my mother is there, you best prepare for the most uncomfortable dinner possible."

I felt Marco's fingers on my hip, under my shirt and jacket. It felt nice to have his fingers on my skin for the moment.

"I assure you, I would like to hold on to what is left of my pride and ego. Having you save me once was enough." Marco said. Part of me wanted him to know I would always save him if he needed it, but I held those words back.

Sasha and my dad left not too long after that, and I didn't try to move in the slightest. Marco's fingers were still resting on my skin even now. Romeao was texting back and forth with someone.

They started speaking in Italian, and I knew it was a conversation I wasn't privy to, but I caught a few words I slightly understood, and the name of Marco's ex-husband was one of them. Instead of agitated, Marco seemed confused.

"Ambrose, might I ask you a small favour?"

"Sure, What do you need?"

"Please head to the nurses' station and have them... or rather ask them politely to remove my ex-husband from my records as my next of kin and emergency contact."

"Are you sure?"

"Yes, I'm positive. We aren't married anymore and both of us are just trying to go about our lives, and frankly, I would rather Theo not know about my medical issues, or have access to records. That isn't his business anymore." His words weren't rude or cruel, they were gentle.

"They might want your signature on some of the paperwork to prove it was your choice to change that information."

"That's fine."

As soon as I stood up, they switched back to Italian, and I wanted in the worst way to know what they were discussing, but I had a decent idea, what or rather, who they were talking about. Theo, his ex-husband. Dragging my hand through my hair, I went to the desk and told them exactly what Marco wanted. They didn't argue or even want him to sign anything. They just removed his ex-husband, and in a moment of my stupidity, when she asked to replace the emergency contact, I gave my name and number.

She never asked for my relationship with him. She probably assumed I was his new partner. Not wanting to make a large issue out of it, I didn't bother fixing it.

Romeao was standing up when I got back into Marco's room, Wren in his arms, looking unhappy.

"I'm going to head to Marco's and put Wren down for his nap. I have some work to do, so there will be another man at Marco's watching Wren when you get there, Ambrose."

"Alright, I'll probably stay here and visit with Marco for a little while longer, then head back to his place." I replied.

"Take your time. There is no rush."

Romeao left with Wren and I spoke. "Is it alright to leave Wren with another person besides Romeao?"

"Romeao only leaves Wren with a few other people, all of whom I know well and have children of their own. Wren is safe with whoever Romeao picked. Come, sit."

"They let me change your information. They didn't seem too worried about it not being your choice."

"Good, Good. Tell me about your night?"

"It was long, and I'm honestly looking forward to your bed." I groaned.

"I also am looking forward to my bed as soon as they let me out of here."

"Marco, you know why dad is only trying to intimidate you, right?"

"I know, and I am going to accept his invitation. Besides, I want to see where you grew up and what your father is like outside of work. Surely he isn't business all the time."

"I told you, it's not him you need to watch. It's my mother. She's crazy at the best of times, and the last thing I want you to witness is her going on her rants."

"Now I have to go. Sounds far too interesting to miss."

"Don't say I didn't at least try to warn you." I chuckled.

Marco took one of my hands and brought it to his lips suddenly, and I narrowed my eyes at him, wondering what he was up to. His lips brushed my knuckles as he spoke.

"Romeao was trying to spare your feelings and our relationship, whatever that might be right now, by speaking in Italian, but he was telling me about Theo. Theo and his partners, or one partner, will stop by at some point when I am home with a care package from Alessio. Frankly, I am unsure why he is actually coming. Anyone else would have been a better choice. We aren't on the best terms, but I think he wants to see with his own eyes I am alright. I can't see another damn reason he would grace my house with his presence again." Marco said, and he looked on edge about the whole thing.

"I will be there, Marco. Even if you just need someone for comfort."

"I did things to Theo that—-"

"I know, you told me, and you have expressed that you're sorry about it and you're changing for your son. You are trying for a better life. He is bringing one or both of his partners for comfort. You have the same chance. Besides, I will probably still be here. I told you, I might not give you back your bed. Your house is quiet and I like that." I said, jokingly again.

"I still don't want you to be involved in the mess I am, But I am finding it increasingly hard to tell myself I need to push you away for your safety."

"Know that if you try even one of the bad things you did to your ex-husband with me, I will make you regret it. He might not have fought back with you, but I will."

Marco looked almost taken aback at my words, and he spoke.

"I would never do to you what I did to Theo. I will never do that to another person. It's not the fair or the appropriate thing to do."

# 18 - Eighteen - Ambrose Grayson's Point Of View.

------------------------------------------------------------

Marco was home at noon today, and Romeao gave us a small heads up that his ex-husband was coming for three. If it was my choice, I would have just told him to leave the shit on the porch and beat feet. Marco was too busy healing, and I wanted to protect him. But Marco didn't like that idea. He said it was a prickly approach when Theo was only being nice. It annoyed me they didn't give Marco a few days to relax at home before they came.

"If you keep pacing like that, you will wake the baby or scare my new friend." Marco chuckled.

"Mochi really does like you, doesn't he?" I chucked. "He's slept on your side of the bed the whole time, too."

Relaxing back on the couch beside Marco, he set his hand on my knee.

"You don't need to stress out about this. You've seen him before, and—-"

"I'm not stressed about me, Marco. I'm stressed on your behalf."

"Well, don't be. He will not want to stay long."

"You hope."

"He won't. He hates this house and everything that happened."

"As if this couldn't be any more awkward." I sighed.

"He has moved on, and I am allowed that too."

I leaned over, watching out for the cat and Marco's wound, and pressed a kiss to his lips.

"If he acts up, I'll drag him out of the house."

"Ambrose."

"I'm being serious. You say the word and I'll just pull him out and—-"

The alarm beeped. Before I could get up, Marco unlocked the door from his phone. They came inside, and they were quiet, but I could shake how uncomfortable I was. Marco leaned over, his voice low and soft.

"No one is looking for a fight, so we should and will be on our best behaviours."

"Understood."

"We let ourselves in, the door was unlocked and I hope that—--" The man in the hallway paused and looked at me, tucked beside Marco on the couch, two men behind him. "I didn't know you would have a guest."

I tried to put space between Marco and me, but he had his hand firmly planted on my knee.

"I unlocked the door to let you in. Ambrose, Theo and his partners, Demitri and Luca." Marco was petting Mochi, not even catching the mildly awkward vibes in the living room.

"Nice to meet you." Theo said, clearly checking me over. He came in, a bag in his hands, and set it on the coffee table. "Alessio packed all kinds of things for you. He included instructions in the bag as well, and some other things, in case the hospital didn't give you much."

Theo and I met eyes, and his eyes weren't soft. I knew it wasn't meant for me when they softened a moment later. They were meant for Marco.

"Can I get you guys anything? A coffee? Water?" I said politely. Marco let go of my knee and I stood up.

"We will all have a coffee. I will lend you a hand." Theo said politely, following me into the kitchen.

While I was pulling down coffee cups, he spoke.

"This has to be pretty awkward for you, too. Romeao, his boss, gave me a heads up. Marco had someone, but to see it is strange. I won't lie, though. I worry about you. Marco is—-"

"Marco isn't your concern. You still somewhere care for him, even if it's because you wanted to make sure he was actually ok, but I've got this. You can focus on moving on and—-"

"Marco told you." He said, mildly shocked.

"Marco was honest about his past, and he told me everything. All the shitty things he did to you, and the abuse."

"I'm glad he was honest with you. For Marco, being honest is a hard thing."

"Marco is trying to better himself for his son."

"Yes. He is, and he is making significant progress at that. He almost seems relaxed, and that's a big thing. After this all blew up and Marco's shit was exposed, it was rough for us all."

"Even though he did what he did, you didn't tell anyone about it. Why?"

"I loved him once. I wanted nothing bad to happen to him. I still don't, but I still don't forgive him either."

"Is it safe to leave Marco with your partners?"

"I hope so. I don't want to see your bad side this soon. You're not his normal type, and it's refreshing. We are all going to bump into each other every now and again, and I just want everything to be normal. Or the most normal that it can be."

"Marco removed you from his emergency information at the hospital." I said, minding my tone, so I didn't sound like I was rubbing it in.

"Good, that's not my job. He has you for that now. I have enough sleepless nights with my two."

He took two cups of coffee for his partners and I took my cup and his and set them on the table.

"Marco, did you want something?" I asked him before sitting down.

"No, Thanks though."

Marco gave me a look, as if he wanted to know what took so long. Theo looked at me and I smiled lightly. Marco spoke.

"Everything alright?"

"Of course. Why wouldn't it be?" I said.

It was one of Theo's partners this time.

"We didn't hear you throwing down in the kitchen, and we all seemed a little concerned. That is all."

"No, we were just having a nice and peaceful conversation about Marco, but that's to be expected." Theo said.

Marco tensed, and I reached over, setting my hand on his knee, like he did to me before, with only him in mind. I wanted to comfort him.

"We were discussing moving on, open and honest."

Marco nodded, and you could tell he was uncomfortable with this conversation still.

"It was mostly good things." Theo said, sipping his coffee.

"I doubt that." Marco said softly and truthfully.

"Actually, it was. I was going to warn Ambrose about your past, but it seems you already did that. The good, the bad and the worst."

"I was open and honest with Ambrose about my past. I even tried to push him away for his own safety." Marco said.

"You need someone to be open and honest with, Marco. Someone you can trust with your life and your needs, and that was never me. Just with Ambrose being here, this house doesn't feel so dark and lonely." Theo said.

"Nothing like what it was last year." His one partner agreed with him.

In the doorway as they were leaving, Theo spoke.

"If you two get serious and to where you get married, I want to be there. I don't hate you Marco, not anymore. Neither of us have time for that. I want to see you happy, as your friend. I want nothing more than to see you actually happy."

Marco was standing up, leaned against the wall, in some pain.

"Thanks. I don't deserve that from you." He said.

"Ambrose, make sure he gets back to the couch and stays relaxed. These mafia men never know when enough is enough." Theo said before closing the door behind him, and Marco groaned.

"I thought he would never leave. He has such a different vibe and makes my skin crawl."

"Marco!"

"What it does! I don't know how either of us thought it was a good idea to get married."

"That's called being in love, and it's not with you." I sighed.

"Good. I don't want him to be in love with me. But on another matter, could you help me back to the couch?"

"Yes, then I'm going to wake the baby."

"Thank you. For everything you've done for me."

"Don't get all mushy on me, Marco." I chuckled as I wrapped my hand around his shoulders to help him back to the couch.

"I feel better, at least a little, that Theo is happy and building a new life with his partners and his daughter."

"I told him you weren't his concern anymore, and that we took him off your health as emergency contact and he said it was my job now to care for you."

"Oh. That's good. At least he knows he doesn't have to worry about my health and—-"

"He said he was happy to see you almost relaxed, and he was pleased that you had been open with me about your past. Mostly, everything he said in the kitchen was good."

"I don't deserve his good words."

I set Marco on the couch and crossed my arms.

"You also don't deserve your bad ones. If you are going to move on completely, you need to let go of this. Theo no longer hates you, he said so himself. He doesn't forgive you, but he wants you to move on."

"Maybe, just maybe, I can allow myself that." Marco said, his eyes meeting mine.

Breaking the silence, I spoke. "What did he mean by I wasn't your usual type?"

"He said that to you?"

"Yes, and he said it was refreshing."

"I went for a type of person who, unlike yourself, only cared about money and appearance, less about the fact I was married and had a partner at home. They were never around longer than I needed them and never would have lifted a finger to help me, emotionally or otherwise."

"Oh. Christ Marco, no wonder you think you deserve nothing."

I set my hand on his cheek.

"Never again, ok. When you need something, emotionally, physically or even mentally, just ask, and I will do my very best to make sure you get that."

# 19 - Nineteen - Ambrose Grayson's Point Of View.

----------

I crossed my arms, a frown set on my face. I couldn't believe he was actually trying this shit right now.

"Ambrose, please. Just help me." Marco said, his voice pained as he tried to put a suit on for dinner.

"Marco, I told you no. Why would you still try this? It hurts, doesn't it?"

"Ambrose. Help me. I am asking nicely."

"No. Pick something else."

"God damn it Ambrose!" Marco yelled, raising his voice at me in frustration and definitely pain.

"If you want my help out of that, you might want to check that tone right back where you got it from, before I decide I didn't see this and leave you like this." I said calmly.

"You wouldn't!"

"I might." I said flatly.

"Fine." Marco hissed, in a bad mood now.

I helped him out of the bit of the suit he had got on. While he swore at me under his breath in Italian, I dug around in his closet to look for something more suitable for his wound and dinner. Since he didn't want to show up in just sweatpants and a sweater, like I was. I didn't have to impress my parents, neither did he, but he was set on it.

I set a nice grey sweater on the bed, and since sweatpants were out of the question, I found a nice pair of deep black jeans.

"You should help me into the suit, Ambrose. This——-"

"No. It's not happening."

"I have an appearance to——-"

"I'm going in sweatpants and a sweater, keep it up, and I'll dress you in the worst things you have in this closet, Marco Di Salvo."

He bit his tongue, words clearly there.

"Smart choice." I muttered.

He dressed in what I picked for him, slowly. He stood up fully when he was dressed and walked to the mirror, and looked over the outfit he put on himself.

"Ambrose, give me back the suit. I will get into it on my own if I must."

"We will be late for dinner. This is enough." I said, before pressing my lips to his and smiling. "Besides, you look less like a Mafia underboss when you're dressed down. I like you dressed down."

"Flirting with me to get me to accept the current situation, huh?" Marco said.

"Eh, it's easier than forcing you to comply with me. Less likely we both will be mad at each other when it's over." I said, smiling at him.

"You think you could force me?"

"I bet I could. You're injured."

"One on one, when I'm healed. If I win, I want you for the night, from sunset to sunrise. Anyway, I choose." Marco said, this devilish look in his eyes.

"Deal. Shake on it?"

He stuck his hand in mine and we did just that, shook on it. I didn't like how his eyes showed a plan there.

"You're not going to kill me, right?" I laughed.

"Hmm, no. It's too late for even that, Ambrose."

"I suppose that's comforting."

"I wouldn't kill you, anyway. You saved my life."

"You would have done it for me, probably."

"Take a knife for you? Or the saving of your life?"

"The saving of my life, Marco. I would never want someone else to take a bullet for me. That's not romantic, it's heartbreaking." I groaned.

"Really? You're not even slightly turned on by that heroic action?"

"God no. How could I be happy knowing that someone else chose to die because they thought my life was more valuable than theirs? I believe that death is peaceful." I said, looking at Marco before speaking again. "Come along. I have to wake Wren and get him ready before we are late."

I watched Marco look in the mirror once more, shaking his head before he followed me out of the room. I went into Wren's room and woke him as he was getting his diaper bag together. Wren was unhappy. He cried, and I tucked his soother into his mouth and held him against me, rubbing his back. I wiped his eyes when he settled down quickly.

"Let's go see daddy." I told him, walking out to the living room.

Marco had the bag and the baby carrier and was holding his side.

"Did you hurt yourself? Do I need to look at it?"

"No. I'll be fine."

"Are you sure?"

"Yes, Ambrose."

"I'll take your word for now."

"You worry too much."

"Did your ex-husband not care if you were injured?"

"I nursed my own wounds, and half the time I said nothing to him. In the end, we weren't living together, so it was easy to pass off as being alright."

"Marco!"

"What? It's the truth. Why would I tell him?"

"I want to know if, when and how you got hurt, and I want to look—-Sorry." I muttered.

"No, please continue. It's refreshing to hear someone cares about me." Marco said, a soft smile on his lips. "But also, hand over my wiggle worm. I want to hold him."

Passing Wren to Marco, he kissed his son's forehead and spoke to him in Italian before doubling back to English.

"Are you sure you want to do this?" I asked.

"Yes. I'm not scared of your dad, and besides, I want to know where you grew up, and all the embarrassing things you've done."

"God. Don't. My mother is going to show you everything."

"Good. I hope so."

"You will regret that." I laughed.

While I buckled and snapped Wren into the car, Marco struggled to get in. I offered to help, but he wasn't feeling accepting of it. Once he was in and settled, I buckled myself in.

"Ready?"

"Yes, drive."

I started the car and backed out of the driveway. Marco looked uncomfortable and was holding his side.

"Nope. You're in pain. We are calling this off." I said.

"Don't you dare. This is important, I need—-"

"You have nothing to prove to my father Marco, you're injured and I won't have you hurt yourself for him."

"I have everything to prove to him, Ambrose. Everything!" He yelled, clearly in pain and annoyed.

"You need not yell about it and the baby is in the car." I replied. He didn't need to be yelling at all, but if he had to, I preferred he didn't do it around Wren.

"Listen, I need to do this. Ok, just trust me. That's all I'm asking. Just trust me, if it's too much, I will let you know." Marco said. Masking the pain that he was definitely in.

I took it easy and drove slowly. His pain was making him very nitpicky and not so nice.

"Must you drive like a damn old lady?" He hissed.

"Must you be a prick about it?" I snapped, without thinking about it.

"Excuse me?" Marco snapped back.

"You heard me. I am driving slow to save you the pain of hitting bumps and holes, and you're being nitpicky about my driving. I don't see the need to speed when I have your son in the fucking car. If I crashed and something happened to him, I wouldn't be alright with that and I would feel terrible."

"You're being fucking dramatic." Marco snapped.

"I am being dramatic? If I'm dramatic, then you're a bloody moron!"

I pulled the car off the road onto the shoulder and got out. Slamming the door and walking a small distance away to get some air. Marco had gotten under my skin with his behaviour and I needed to get out of the enclosed space with him, so that I didn't punch him. I wasn't known for violence at all, but he was pushing it. If that happened, and I hit him, I would never forgive myself for that. It was a chance I wasn't willing to take.

After a few deep breaths of the cool air, I pulled my hand through my hair and walked back to the car. Opening the door, I got back inside and put my seatbelt back on. Marco was quiet in the passenger seat most of the rest of the way to my dads, only saying something once we got into town, about wanting to grab something for dessert for my parents.

Stopping at a grocery store, I handed the keys to Marco and left the car running.

"I'll run in and grab them something. You just stay here."

"Spare no expenses." Marco said, handing me his credit card.

"Yeah, yeah. Understood."

Getting out, I headed inside and grabbed a small fancy cheese cake with loads of fresh fruit and a bottle of wine at the little store inside the grocery store on the way out. I set both on the floor behind Marco's seat.

At my parents' house, Marco again refused to let me help him. I knew this was a moment of pride for him, and he didn't want to need my help in front of my parents. But I was more concerned about his health than his pride and ego. We were slightly late when we got inside. Dad took Wren instead of the wine and cheesecake from Marco.

"Here, let me get that——--"

"Ambrose Grayson, you're late for dinner again." I heard my mother say, from wherever she was.

"Yeah. That's——--"

"That's my fault, Mrs Grayson." Marco said politely, covering my ass and holding out the wine and cheesecake as she crept out from the kitchen with a look on her face.

"Your father said you were bringing someone to dinner, but I thought he was spouting nonsense again." My mother said, taking the wine and cake from Marco and thanking him for it.

Mom and Marco went to the kitchen, and I met dad in the living room. He had Wren out of the car seat and propped up in the couch's corner as he fixed his clothing and then tickled him. Counter-productive if you asked me, but he seemed like he was having a blast with Wren.

I cleared my throat, and he turned around.

"Oh, it's just you."

"Who did you think it was?"

"Marco, looking for his spawn."

"He is with mother."

"Ah, Your mother hasn't even spotted the baby yet."

"Give it a few minutes." I said.

"You look stressed out, Ambrose."

"It was a rough ride. Marco gets nitpicky when he's in pain, but he wouldn't let me cancel the dinner. You know, pride and ego."

"I understand. He thinks I invited him here to rough him up, or whatever parents do to their children's partners, but I'm not about that. You know this. I leave that up to your mother, and from the sounds of the chit chatting, she likes him."

"I know dad, I tried to tell him he had nothing to prove to you, but he kept going on about having something to prove. Yet little does he know, it's not you to worry about, it's the she-devil in there." I said lowly, laughing and pointing to the kitchen.

The sound of footsteps coming to the living room meant Marco had no doubt told my mother about poor sweet little Wren and she was coming to claim him from my father.

"She's coming to steal the baby."

"I hope not. I like him." Dad said, tickling him some more.

"Me too." I mumbled, looking at his small little face, his giggles making me happy too.

# 20 - Twenty - Ambrose Grayson's Point Of View.

My mother snatched Wren up from my dad without so much as a word about it and showered him with affection. I couldn't say this surprised me, though. This was normal for her. Marco didn't seem to have a problem with her behaviour, but I did.

"Mom, you shouldn't kiss other people's babies. More so without the parents' permission." I hissed.

"I'm sure Marco's fine with it." She said dismissively.

She went to kiss Wren again, and I covered where she went to kiss with my hand.

"Ambrose!"

"I think you should stop kissing him. He is not your child and you could make him sick."

She was visibly mad now. "You only say that because of your job. I'm not bothering you."

"You could make him sick. And you never asked Marco if he was comfortable with you kissing his child."

"Ambrose." Marco said softly, unaware that this was a hill I would happily die on when it comes to my mother.

"He is not your child, Ambrose. You don't get a say. I'm sure if Marco had an issue with me kissing his child, he would say something." She said, emphasis on that it was his child and not mine. It instantly rubbed me in ways I couldn't handle and Dad knew that, too. He took me by the arm, yanking me with him to the kitchen, claiming he needed my help.

I could hear Marco and mom chatting in the living room, as dad was speaking to me.

"Ambrose, please. I know her words were unkind, just take a deep breathe——-"

"She doesn't need to behave that way, and Marco won't say anything to her because he's under the impression that he needs to impress you." I groaned. "If I knew Marco could drive safely, I'd drink myself into a coma just to make this night go by faster."

"Ambrose!"

"I won't. I swear. At least not knowing I have to drive Marco and Wren home."

"I know your mother is hard to deal with sometimes."

"Understatement. I swear, I don't know how you do it."

"When you fall in love, and love someone, you become blind to even their worst behaviours." Dad said, smiling softly. "You will understand sooner than later, I'm sure."

Dad checked the food in the oven and cleared his throat, and I looked to the doorway. Marco was holding his side, but keeping a straight face.

"Hi, am I interrupting?"

"No, are you ok?"

"Oh, this yeah, I just got up at an angle." He said. Dad left us for the baby and I crossed my arms.

"Alright, let me have a look."

"No, I'm alright, really. But are you ok?"

"Yeah. Nothing I'm not used to. But seriously, let me look, I don't want to get rough and force you to show me, But I will if I have too."

"Fine."

I had Marco lean against the counter and I moved his pants down, and grabbed my phone, using the flashlight to have a better look at the spot where the bandage was lifting. Getting on my knees to look at the wound, without removing anymore of the tape, I used the flashlight to get a good look. It looked like it was healing and didn't have any puss or signs of infection. The stitches looked a little tight, though.

"Really Ambrose! In my fucking kitchen!" I heard my mother scream, startling me and I jumped, touching Marco's wound and he let out a hiss.

"Shit, Marco, I'm so fucking sorry. Hold on, let me make sure I didn't make any of this worse." I said, moving the bandage while my mother came around the counter to see exactly what was going on.

"Are you injured?" She asked.

"It's just a slight wound." He muttered.

"He was stabbed." I hissed, really looking over his wound now. He looked down at me and frowned.

"You could have cancelled dinner. I would have understood." She said politely, like she didn't expect me to be here, alive or dead. "Let me go get the first aid kit. Maybe there's something in there that's useful to you."

She walked off, and I looked up at him.

"What?" He asked.

"She likes you. She gave you a pass. I don't even get that. I could be dying and she would still expect me to be here for dinner."

She returned and set the first aid kit on the counter. "If you need to rest, Ambrose can show you to his room, and you're more than welcome to stay the night if needed. Ambrose can run out and get a playpen from one of the stores for here."

"Thank you." Marco said politely before she rushed back out to the living room to spend time with Wren again.

"If you need to rest, please let me know and I'll show you to my room and——"

"Are you sure you can handle staying here the night if I need that?"

"For you, yes."

"Wren has most things he needs, and I——"

"I'll make sure Wren and you are looked after. I'll go get him a playpen here, and while I'm at the store, I'll grab you something. The spare clothing I have here won't fit you."

"Are you positive? I can handle you driving us home——"

"No, I'd rather not chance anything. We are staying here."

He nodded, and I opened the kit, finding clean gloves and bandages. I replaced his, and tossed everything into the garbage. He grabbed my arm after I readjusted all his clothing and made sure he was pretty much comfortable.

"Did you need something more?" I asked.

"Yes."

What is it you need?"

"A kiss. Maybe two." He whispered, licking his lips as he looked at mine.

"I suppose I can do that for you."

"Good, I am in no condition to be demanding and following up my demands for a kiss."

I closed the space between us, being careful to watch his wound and pressed my lips to his, the taste of my mother's peach iced tea lingering on his lips still.

"Mmm, you taste sweet, just like mom's iced tea." I muttered, laughing lightly.

"Yes, she gave me a glass. It was refreshing."

"It's one of the best things she makes. Trust me."

Marco tucked his arm around me and pulled me close again, kissing me. The kiss was gentle and needy, but Marco was the one who pulled away first. "I will repay you for all your care and concern once I'm healed. You have my word."

"You don't have to give me your word, and you don't have to repay me. My care and concern is because I like you, Marco. It's normal when you love—It's normal ha-ha."

I put space between us and dragged my hand through my hair. I couldn't believe I almost told him I loved him in slightly more complex words than just, I love you.

"I'm going to get the stuff from the store, so I'll—--"

"Take my card, please."

"Marco, I can pay."

"No, this is nonnegotiable. I'm paying for my child and I."

"No. I can."

"But you won't, because I am paying. Don't argue with me. I will go with you if I need to make sure you're going to use my card."

"No, it's fine."

Dad entered the kitchen, Wren in his arms, sleeping.

"Your mom said you guys might be staying. If you want to get a playpen from the store, my credit card is on the—--"

"No need, I'll pay, I don't mind." Marco said firmly.

"Alright then, if you're sure." Dad said, as Marco pulled out his card and gave it to me.

"I'm very sure. I will pay for my child and I. Thank you for the offer though." Marco said politely. Marco pulled me closer, leaning down to whisper into my ear. "Get anything you need, too. I will pay for you too, of course, Tesoro (Darling)."

The soft Italian word at the end of his words sent shivers down my spine, and I hoped it was a good name and not something bad. I was going to have to look it up the minute I got into the car. I was curious about it. Making sure I had everything, I went out to the car and quickly made a list on my phone about all the things I was going to need to buy. I set to looking up the word he called me. Tesoro.

I butchered the spelling, but I was able to find the word. Sitting there, with the knowledge he called me darling, in his own native tongue was interesting. It left a fluttering in my chest and I gave my head a damn shake. It was far too early to have feelings for this man. Far too early.

Driving to the store, I was on autopilot the entire time. I found everything on the list. Paid with Marco's card and left. Maddox's car was in the driveway when I pulled back in. Abandoning everything in Marco's SUV. I went inside first. Marco and my mom were in the living room with Wren. I took a deep breath, and Marco spoke.

"Need help with the stuff?"

"No, no. I've got it, I just saw Maddox's car and—--"

"He's talking business with your father. Something happened tonight." Marco said, my mother ignoring his words, to focus on playing with the baby. It was rare for mom to be home when Maddox came by. I wasn't even sure if mom knew what Maddox did for a job. Or how involved dad was with it.

Heading back out to the car, I grabbed the stuff and closed the truck, locking the door. Inside, Marco took the single bag, and I refused to let him take the box with the playpen inside. I didn't need him hurting himself.

"Oh, Ambrose, you can leave the playpen down here. Your dad and I will be up well before you will, and Marco is injured so. We can look after him if he cries."

"Alright, that sounds like a good idea." Marco said.

I looked at Marco and he smiled softly at me, and I set the playpen down and Mom shewed me away, saying my dad could handle setting it up. Following Marco up the stairs, I frowned and once we got into my room; I closed the door.

"Why did you let her keep the baby down there? Are you actually alright with——-"

"Ambrose, quiet."

"Marco."

"If your mother wants to spend time with Wren, I'm ok with it. I'm glad she likes him."

"Don't let her overstep with him, though."

"If she does, I'll tell her."

I frowned deeper. Worried that he wouldn't tell her. He set the bag on my bed and looked around. Pausing to look at the wall of pictures, mostly just dad and I doing things together.

"You two are close."

"Yes, he was the one who was around all the time. He is the one I go to when I need something, like parental support or advice."

"I hope Wren and I have the relationship you two have." Marco said, softly.

Even though I heard every word he said, about wanting Wren and him to have the relationship dad and I have. I realized I wanted the kind of love that my parents have with him.

"I want the kind of relationship my parents have." I muttered. Marco paused, his eyes on me, and I felt my face heat up.

"What was that?"

"Nothing, I was just muttering to myself."

"Hmm, I could have sworn you just said that you want the kind of relationship that your parents have. Is that what you said, Ambrose?" Marco asked, backing me into the door.

"Wait! You're injured. We shouldn't—-" Marco pressed his lips to mine and when he pulled away, he smiled softly. "Rain check for when I can make you understand."

"O—ok."

# 21 - Twenty - One - Ambrose Grayson's Point Of View.

- - - - - - - - - - - - - - - - - - - - - - - - - - - - - - - - - - - - - - - - - - - - -

Maddox was gone when dad came to get us for dinner. He looked stressed out, so while mom was still in the living room, I asked.

"It's bad. Whatever Maddox came to tell you, isn't it?"

"It's not good. That's for sure." Dad said, before glancing at Marco.

"Did you want me to go check on your wife? And the baby?" He asked politely.

"No, I'm sure Romeao will be making you aware of the situation shortly as well, so I guess me telling you or talking about around you isn't going to make a difference."

"Alright. I'm all ears then."

"Maddox came to alert me that his men found a few bodies that didn't belong to them or their activities and they are concerned that there is an active serial killer on the loose. Alexi ran the faces of some of the newer bodies, and they were from all over the place. All from our district, but from all the towns."

"Yikes. What does he want done about it?" I asked.

"He's asked us to do our jobs and find this person. He's willing to lend us anything we need to make this quicker, but he is concerned that it will shed light on his illegal activities."

"Yes, the news of a serial killer will attract unwanted attention." Marco said, looking concerned himself now. Pulling a hand through his hair, he looked at me. "Please be extra careful while you're working."

"Of course. I have no interest in being the next victim of a killer."

"I doubt anyone does." My dad said, frowning intensely.

"Eh, you never know. There are some freaks out there." I said flatly. My dad shook his head and went and fetched my mother. I sighed, and Marco smiled softly at me. I liked it more than I cared to admit at the moment.

"They like Wren." I whispered.

"Good, I'm glad."

I liked Wren too.

Dad came back, Mom right behind him with Wren in her arms, her smile large and genuine. Dad and I brought all the food to the table, along with all the plates and utensils to serve it. While mom and Marco chatted, Marco ate while holding Wren and feeding him, too. I watched him the entire time, too distracted by his parenting to really eat. He looked at me while feeding a chunk of chicken to Wren.

"I should have bought a high chair." I hummed.

"We can get one another time. I'm sure this is not the last time Marco and Wren will come for dinner." My mother said, her eyes shining with glee.

"Of course Wren and I would be happy to come back for dinner, as long as we are welcome to join Ambrose."

Dinner finished not long after, and Marco helped my mother with the playpen and getting Wren ready for bed. Marco put Wren down for bed, and we were practically shewed away by my mother to my spare room. She claimed to have things under control and assured us we should turn in for the night. Marco chuckled when he closed the door behind us.

"I think I might have to fight your mother for my child back."

"She probably is thinking that this is the closest to a grandchild she will have and wants to savour it."

"You don't want children?" Marco asked suddenly.

"Maybe, but not alone. I want the entire family unit. Two parents and some fortunate children with good childhoods."

"Hm."

"What?"

"Just trying to find where Wren and I fit. If you will have us, that is."

I was speechless and without really thinking about it; I wrapped my arms around Marco and held him against me.

"I will always have Wren and you. Even if you get sick of me, Marco."

He chuckled and hugged me tighter, flinching but not letting go.

"Marco, please don't hurt yourself just to entertain me."

"I'm not. Yes, it hurts, but not more than if I let go and don't fill my need to have you right here in my arms."

"If you weren't injured, that might have talked me out of my pants and shirt." I muttered.

"I can still do that if you want me too, Ambrose." Marco smirked.

"You offered me a raincheck. I will take you up then. When you can properly talk me out of my pants, Marco Di Salvo."

"I will accept that."

"Good, you better."

We both stripped down, and laid in the bed after Marco flicked off the bedroom light and turned on his phone flashlight. Together on the bed, I laid in Marco's arms, just enjoying the heat from his body and the scent of his cologne.

"We should do this more often. It's nice just to have you in my arms." Marco whispered into the dark, and I found myself smiling softly.

"I agree. Just the two of us enjoying each other."

"It's honestly so peaceful. It's been so long since I've been this content with my own life, and you're the reason for that Ambrose." Marco confessed.

"Don't say things like that Marco, I'll never want to go back to my apartment."

"You don't have to, Ambrose. My house is large enough for you and Mochi. Somehow, I don't think it would thrill him to have to give up his spot on the bed to go home. We've bonded." Marco chuckled.

"Haha, Mochi would be thrilled to know you like him so much." I laughed.

"Does it thrill you to know I like you that much too, Ambrose?" He asked softly, and I felt my cheeks heat up.

"Yes." I whispered, unsure at that moment if this was the right time to let him on to the fact that I was falling for his charms, and that beautiful Italian accent. Marco pulled me closer to him and his lips pressed against my temple.

If this was bliss, I wanted to stay here in this moment forever.

Marco passed out quickly, and I watched him for a while. Slipping out of his arms and heading back downstairs, after pulling my shirt back on. Mom was sitting on the couch when I came downstairs. She was watching Wren sleep, and she looked at me in the dark.

"Is it serious with you two, Ambrose?"

Sitting down on the couch, I spoke. "I really hope so."

"I hope you mean that. While you were at the store, all he talked about was you and wanting to know you better."

"Really?"

"Yes, his eyes lit up too while we spoke about you. He is clearly more interested in more than just your body, Ambrose."

"I am definitely attached to more than his body. The thought of Mochi and I having to leave his house is depressing." I said absentmindedly.

"Are you staying with him?"

"Yes, I have been for a little while."

"Permanently?"

"No, I still have my apartment, but I don't really think I want to go back. His bed is comfortable, and his——----"

"Ambrose, you're enjoying it more than just his house. You're enjoying his company."

"Yes, I've fallen in love with Marco. I won't deny that."

"Your father isn't honest with me about his work friends, but I know what they all do. I'm not stupid. I just don't feel the need to get involved. Don't lie to me when I ask you, is Marco also one of your fathers 'work friends' Ambrose?" She said, flatly.

"Yes, he is, but not part of the family dad interacts with the most." I answered honestly.

"I have no right to butt in and tell you how to live your life anymore, and I can see he wants to be with you. But I want you to be careful." She said, giving me a weird look.

"You've never backed off like this in my life before. Why now?"

"This is really the first time you've brought home someone, and it just really set in you're an adult and you're starting your own family now." She said, looking at Wren sleeping soundly in the playpen. She looked back at me and spoke. "Now, go back to your lover and leave me with the baby in peace."

I shook my head as I stood up and trekked back up the stairs to my room. Opening the door, I slipped into the room, closing the door without waking up Marco. I did, however, accidentally wake him when I slipped back into the bed.

"Where did you go?" He mumbled, his voice filled with sleep.

"Down to check on the baby." I whispered, snuggling close to him.

"Mm, how'd that go?"

"I talked with my mother for a few moments before she chased me off to watch the baby sleep in peace."

He mumbled something, but I didn't catch it as he went back to sleep and I listened to him breathe softly for a few minutes before snuggling deeper against him and closing my eyes. Only time would tell if we could work together as partners, lovers even.

I woke up later to the sound of Wren crying and I tried to get up, but Marco wrapped his arm around me.

"He's ok. Your parents are looking after him. This is the second time he's cried. They handled it the first time. They know we are here if they need us." He whispered.

"Did you wake up the first time he cried?" I asked, rolling in his arms to face him.

"Yes, I listened to see if he would go back to sleep."

"Hm."

"I also laid here and watched you sleep. You looked very peaceful, sleeping away, Ambrose."

"I did that last night, with you." I muttered, laying my head on his shoulder, and taking a deep breath of him. "I miss our bed." I muttered, without really thinking twice about it.

"Our bed?" Marco questioned, and I was suddenly way more away than I wanted to be at realizing my mistake.

"Yeah, our bed. You're stuck with me now." I said, laughing to make it seem like playful banter and not a slip of my tongue.

"Our bed is where we left it, and we will be back there soon."

# 22 - Twenty - Two - Ambrose Grayson's Point Of View.

------------------------------------------------------

Marco wasn't in bed when I woke up, but he had tucked his pillow against me to keep me in the snug position I had been in. Stretching in the bed, Marco's scent was comforting. Getting out of bed, I was craving Marco's touch.

Pulling a sweater out of my closet, it still fit, and I had a little laugh. The grey LHPD sweater looked funny on me, but I had dozens of them. I got them from dad all the time, since he had dozens of them too. The only person I knew that activity wore them was Lukas, and maybe Sasha.

Heading downstairs, Mom's car was gone, and I frowned. Chances were, she had probably left for work again. It wasn't uncommon.

Wren was sleeping in the playpen, a bottle beside him. Little man was milk drunk and sleeping now. I smiled softly, watching him sleeping. Content, I walked to the kitchen. Dad and Marco were just chatting over coffee, and I couldn't help but laugh a little. The chief of police, and the underbosses of Romeao's family, just drinking coffee together.

Sneaking up on Marco, just as I was about to wrap my arms around him, he spoke.

"Good morning, Ambrose."

"How did you know that I was coming?" I groaned.

"The sound of your feet on the floor." He chuckled.

"Morning dad." I said to dad, before leaning down and pressing my lips to Marco's right there, in front of him. "You taste like coffee, Mr Di Salvo." I hummed before walking to make my coffee.

"How did you sleep?" Dad asked, just leaving the question hanging.

"Good, till Marco left me."

"I left you in bed two hours ago." He said.

"Ugh. You could have woken me up."

"I didn't want to wake you up. You need your sleep," Marco replied.

"Where's mom?" I asked.

"She got called in just after I got up," Marco said.

"She had to fly out. Another company needs her help. She was all over it. So they must've offered her good money," Dad said, getting up and starting breakfast. "Anything you want for breakfast, Ambrose?"

"Hmm. Pancakes? Is that ok with you, Marco?"

"I'll accept anything. Thank you." Marco said politely.

"You don't have to be so polite, Marco. We are both off duty here. Here, you are just my son's boyfriend?" He said, questioning what we were.

"You are the father of my boyfriend. That demands respect alone." Marco said.

My dad chuckled and looked at me. "Ambrose's mother is the one you need to watch out for, not me, Marco."

"Mrs Grayson has been a lovely host. I would like to think she likes me, or at least my child, and that wins me some points."

Sipping my coffee, I chuckled before going to sit down in the spot beside Marco and setting my hand on his thigh. Making sure dad was busy at the counter.

"You're misbehaving, Ambrose." Marco whispered.

"Yes. But I missed your touch."

"Patience, Ambrose." Marco scolded me, and I exhaled.

I heard my dad snicker from behind the counter, and he turned around. "I have no clue what you're talking about, but from that sound, he told you no."

"How'd you know?" I asked, knowing the answer.

"That's your 'no' sigh. You make it every time someone says no to you."

"I never noticed. I will have to pay attention to that." Marco chuckled.

"I'm heading for a shower." I said.

"Take Marco to. Conserve some water." My dad said, before going back to whisking up a bunch of eggs.

"Marco, come along. Let's not waste water."

Marco finished his coffee and followed behind me upstairs after checking on Wren, who was still passed out in the playpen, having the best nap of his life, no doubt. I was almost jealous of it. That kid got fantastic sleep.

Heading to the bathroom, I pulled Marco with me. I closed the door behind us and headed to the bath and shower combo, reaching to turn the water on. Setting it at a decent temperature. I checked it again and pulled the shower curtain closed.

I turned around and Marco pulled me against him, pressing his lips to mine.

"I wonder what one of us will cave in for the other's touch first." He whispered against my lips.

Marco was teasing me. I knew he was, but my body reacted. He was purposely winding me up. He stepped back and started stripping his clothing off. I watched him until he dropped his boxers on the floor and slipped his fingers under my shirt. Pulling it off, he threw it to the side and stepped closer again. He grabbed my hips and pulled me against him, pressing his body against mine. I felt every inch of his skin, and my heart raced faster. His lips moved against mine as he whispered, "I know you want me." His breath tickled my lips as he said it, and I couldn't deny it. I felt my face flush, and I wanted to kiss him even more.

"Marco, You're terrible." I whined.

"And you're not, Amore? You were touching me in the kitchen, with your father present."

"Hush, I have no clue what you mean." I chuckled.

"Sure you don't," Marco said, as he shoved my bottoms down, and used his foot so I could step out of them. I stepped into the spray first so that Marco's dressings didn't get soaked.

"Just don't get completely wet, and I'll change your dressings the minute we get out, and then at home, I'll change it to a waterproof cover."

"Home, huh?"

"Slip of the tongue." I muttered.

I covered Marco's bandages with my dry hands, while he quickly washed and then rinsed. He switched me spots.

"You can get out, if you want–" Marco's arms wrapped around my waist, and his right hand slipped down my hip, and he grabbed my cock. "Oh. Hmm." I said, finishing my sentence.

"I'm sure you don't want me to leave, Ambrose." The way he said my name was thick with his accent, and I was sure that was the part that clouded my judgement, not his hand around the base of my cock.

"Marco." I hissed.

"Relax a little." He whispered, pressing his lips to my shoulder, and moving his hand. His touch was electric, sending sparks through my body, and my skin was on fire. I knew I should pull away, but I felt like I was in a trance, and I could not move. His voice was like a drug, and his words were an invitation I could not refuse. I wanted to feel his touch, and I wanted to stay in his arms. I relaxed back against him a little.

"Please tell me if you're in any pain at all, Marco, seriously."

"Shh, just let me help you get off, Ambrose."

"This is a terrible idea." I grunted.

"Just listen to me. I'm older."

"Does not mean you're wiser, trust me."

He tightened his hand around my cock, and I hissed. He loosened his grip, and they slowly started to jack me off. Marco's hand moved faster, and I felt the sensation building inside me. His grip was gentle, but firm, and he knew exactly how to touch me. I could feel my orgasm building, and I let out a moan as I felt my body trembling with pleasure. Marco's hand moved faster, and I felt my orgasm coming. I let out a moan as I felt my body being taken over with pleasure. I felt myself spilling over, and I felt Marco's hand slow to a stop. I was completely spent, and I slumped against him for a few moments. Marco kissed my shoulder, and I felt his smile against my skin. He brought his hand up and licked it.

I made a face, and he chuckled.

"I'd tell you not to be salty, but from the taste of it, you're pretty salty."

"Ugh, Marco, now is not the time for semen jokes." I groaned at him.

"I thought it was the perfect time, actually."

Marco got out, and I quickly washed my hair and body before getting out. Marco had the first aid kit already sitting out, and was sitting on the toilet waiting in a fresh pair of boxers. I dried off, pulling the towel around my hips, and wiped my hands again for good measure before fighting with the gloves. I got down on my knees to be at the appropriate height.

Redressing his wound, Marco was cupping his cock, and I chuckled. "Guess you're just as bad as me, huh?"

"You're on your knees in front of me, Ambrose, kind of hard to shut my cock and balls off."

"I could help with that, but I would be worried about you jerking and ripping stitches, so you will have to suffer with the hard cock until it goes away, Marco darling."

"Kiss me, at the very least." He said, pulling me to him so he could kiss me. Standing up, the towel dropped to the floor and Marco pinched my left ass cheek, and I hissed.

"Hey." I hissed.

"Firm ass, very nice." He hummed. "Your uniform does a really marvellous job of hugging that ass. You rock that uniform."

"You told me to have patience, yet you're flirting with me, like you're not being held together with stitches, so your insides don't coat the bathroom floor." I scolded him.

"Fair enough." He laughed, standing up, and leaving the bathroom, following me to the bedroom. I pulled on a pair of new boxers and laid back on the bed. Marco straddled my hips and pinned me to the bed. I took this time to fix the wrinkle that had formed in his bandage, and he hissed.

"I'm positive you just ripped out the remaining hair I had there."

"You will live. It's only hair, Marco."

# 23 - Twenty - Three - Ambrose Grayson's Point Of View.

-------------------------------------------------------------

A bit later, Marco and I set off to head back to his place, and when we got there, Mochi was a furious cat. He was sitting on the side of the couch, screaming his face off.

"I know, I know. Sorry, I'll feed you now." I said, hold my hands up. Wren was tucked into the side of Marco's neck. He had slept the entire way back home and was miserable again when Marco woke him up.

I cracked a can of cat food open and fed him. He quieted down then because he was too busy stuffing his face with shredded chicken and rice. Marco had put Wren into a play saucer and he was touching all the toys, still looking miserable. Marco wore a similar look on his face as he stretched out on the couch.

"You two are sharing the same face today." I chuckled, leaning over the back of the couch to look at him.

"You should take time off work until we figure out who this killer is, Ambrose." Marco said.

"Sounds great, but no. I can't do that. Mia and I both need the money."

Marco clicked his tongue in annoyance, and I reached down and brushed a piece of hair from his face.

"I'll be careful though."

His look said he didn't believe me, which was alright because I didn't really believe myself either.

"If anything happens to you, you best hope you're dead before I get my hands on you——-"

"Oh, hush." I muttered, slipping two of my fingers into his mouth. His teeth locked onto my fingers and I grunted. He didn't let go either. His tongue was lapping at the ends of my fingers, while those teeth of his bit into my flesh. I used my free hand to cup his chin, and he let go of my fingers. "You're lucky you're injured, Marco."

"Am I?"

"Yes, I have a craving to fuck you, deeply." I said, lowering my voice.

He chuckled. "You'll have to wait."

"It seems I will. But, that's alright. I'll be patient, and it will be worth the wait." I whispered. Looking up, I watched mini Marco playing with all his toys, and he looked far less miserable now. "He's too cute."

Marco's phone rang, and he sighed. Fishing it out of his pocket, he answered. "Hello, Marco speaking."

Whoever was on the other line was speaking rapidly, and Marco pinched between his eyebrows.

"Mark. Just handle things like you normally do for him. He will see to that when he returns."

He rattled out a bunch more words before Marco pulled the phone away from his ear. "Just once, I would like things to stay functioning while I am away. Mark is Romeao's caretaker if you want to give him a title. He gets along with him well, and cooks, cleans, and does lord knows what else for Romeao."

"Was that the man who was here looking after Wren?" I asked.

"Possibly. Mark is one of the few people Romeao and I don't mind allowing near Wren."

Wren was giggling as he bounced around in the baby saucer. Marco reached up and tilted my chin down. "Pay attention to me, Ambrose, we were speaking."

"Sorry, Wren's little giggles caught my attention." I admitted.

He dropped his hand, and I moved around the couch to the arm, leaning down and pressing my lips to his. "Here comes your cat, Marco." I laughed, hearing Mochi's bell as he came running over. He was seeking Marco.

"He likes me." Marco smiled.

"He has good taste in men." I muttered, messing up his dark hair with my fingers. Mochi jumped up on Marco's legs and inched only close enough so that Marco would pet him. I had to head back to work tonight, and I wasn't super thrilled about it.

"I have to head to work tonight, around seven or eight."

"Call in."

"Marco I can't. I know how you feel about the issues going on, but I still have a job to do, like you do." I muttered.

"Quit it then. You can—--"

"Marco. We can discuss your dislike for my job later, maybe when I get back around seven a.m."

"Tsk. Even a day shift would be better."

"Couple weeks, and I'll be back to day shift again." I smiled, ruffling his hair again. Stepping away from him, he sighed.

"I'm going to look for something to make for lunch."

Heading to the kitchen, I opened the fridge and looked for something easy. Sandwiches looked to be the best idea, so I went with that. Pulling all the stuff out, I went back to the living room to get the baby, and Marco and Mochi were both passed out on the couch.

Wren hardly made a sound when I pulled him out of the saucer and took him to the kitchen, and sat him in the highchair. I gave him a couple of small pieces of some different things to eat and watched him eat. I waited until he had everything chewed and nothing he could choke on before I left the room to wake Marco. He woke up almost right away and groaned.

"I pulled out things for lunch. Are you hungry? Do you need a hand up?"

Marco hummed, and I helped him up. He followed behind me to the kitchen, Mochi behind him. "Marco, you stole my cat."

"And your point?" He hummed, reaching his hand down after he sat down, and Mochi ran to his hand to give him affection.

"My cat is openly stealing my man." I sighed.

"Your man? Is that what I am?" Marco said, his eyes scanning me.

Not sure what to say, I just hummed. But Marco didn't seem to like that much at all. He snagged my arm when I set down the plate of food in front of him.

"Ambrose."

"Eat lunch. I have to feed the baby more." I said, not looking at him directly.

"Ambrose?"

I looked down, and Marco yanked me towards me. "If I am your man, Ambrose, what does that make you to me?"

I blinked, and then stupidly smiled at him. "That's for you to decide. Just know I'm like a stray cat. It will be hard for you to get rid of me now."

Marco chuckled and watched me as I went back to feed Wren more pieces of things. Marco was feeding Mochi a small sliver of cheese. "That's why he likes you, Marco."

"Whatever works." Marco replied.

I made myself a sandwich after giving mini Marco more food too. And paced the kitchen.

"Ambrose, sit and eat."

"I will." I muttered, but still paced.

"Sit and eat, now." His voice had a very interesting tone to it. Was that his dad voice?

Sitting down, he thanked me. I picked at my food and was all too aware of Marco watching me.

"Don't worry about this. It's normal. I have a lot I'm thinking about." I laughed, ripping another piece off the sandwich and chewing it. I was worried about Marco and Wren, the gangs, and this new apparent serial killer. It was taking up a fair bit of my brain, too.

He stood up on his own and took my empty plate when I was done. "I'm making us each another sandwich."

"No, no. Let me." I said, trying to get up, but Marco just set his hand on my shoulder and applied a little pressure.

"I'm fine to do this, Ambrose. This is far from the first time, or the last time, I'll be wounded."

A frown set on my face, and let out a sigh. "How do you deal with it? I could never."

"Practice." he said, smiling. Heading to the counter to make us each another sandwich, and give Wren more chunks of food. I watched him and smiled. I could grow to enjoy this. He set the plate down in front of me and paused. "Ambrose?"

"Hmm?" I said, looking up at him. He slipped his right hand under my chin and pressed a kiss to my lips. "If you never leave my house, I'd be ok with that."

A smile formed on my lips. "Remember that, because each day I spend here, I don't want to leave."

He sat down, and his face showed discomfort, but he didn't voice it. Instead, I picked at the second sandwich and he frowned. "Has your eating always been like this?"

"Picking at food, you mean?" I asked, shoving a bite of food into my mouth.

"Yes."

"Yeah, but it's nothing to be concerned about. It's just something I do."

"As long as you eat enough." Marco hummed.

"Are you concerned about me, mister big bad mafia underboss?" I teased him.

"I am generally concerned about you, Ambrose. I'll try to have more meals with you." Marco said, and I frowned. "You're worried about my eating habits. I do eat."

"I see that," Marco said.

"If it would make you feel better, I wouldn't turn down having more meals with you. Besides, you're not heading back to work for a little while, so we have the chance."

After we finished eating, Marco took Wren for his nap, and I stretched out on the couch. Mochi jumped up on my chest and knocked the air out of me. I didn't complain. I took the love he was offering me.

Marco stretched out when he left Wren's room, his arms above his head and his lower torso, and hips, and the dark hair that was littered there was visible as his shirt rode up.

"How sinful." I muttered, wanting to touch him.

"Come." Marco said, walking to the bedroom and stopping in the doorway. "You could use a nap before you head to work."

"Could I?" I smiled lazily, getting up off the couch disturbing Mochi in the process. "Cat's not going to like you now." I laughed.

"He is welcome in the bed, too." Marco said, leaving the bedroom door open, and carefully taking off his clothing and getting changed. Without thinking it through, I touched the patch of hair on his lower torso.

"Ambrose."

"Hmm?" I said, looking up at him.

"Your hand?"

"My hand..." I looked down and removed my hand. "Right. Sorry. Hard to keep my hands off you. Good looking man and all that. Plus, you showed it to me earlier." I huffed as I pulled off my pants and crawled into the bed.

Marco found a new lighter T-shirt before he joined me in bed, in his boxers and his torso covered. Once that wound was healed, I was going to have to convince this man that the shirt needed to go. It was only in my way.

# 24 - Twenty - Four - Ambrose Grayson's Point Of View.

---

"Ambrose."

"No." I grunted, and stuffed my face further into his ribs, the spicy scent of his tickling my nose.

"You have work soon."

"Ugh, I should have called in." I groaned. Sitting up, I hated it. I fell back against the bed and snuggled back into Marco's side. "If I get fired, I get fired."

Marco wasn't having it, and actually got out of the bed, and I didn't have a choice but to get up then. "Marco, I thought you liked me." I whined.

"I do. That's why I'm going to feed you dinner before I send you to work."

I followed him to the kitchen, stretching out. "I'll get Wren." I muttered. I wanted baby cuddles before work.

Mochi was in the crib with him, and he was awake. But didn't cry. He was too busy with Mochi, who was grooming his little tufts of hair.

Stealing Wren from Mochi, I took him to the kitchen. He smiled at Marco when he saw him. He got all wiggly, and Marco and I swapped. I took the large spoon from him, and he took my wiggly baby.

Mochi made his way into the kitchen and meowed. He touched Wren's head before he made a disgusted face. "Why is his head so damp?"

"Mochi was performing his fatherly duties of grooming the naked kitten." I snorted.

"Sweet. But also disgusting. I didn't expect him to be damp."

"Mochi loves little Wren." I chuckled.

"Good. I'm glad your child likes mine." Marco muttered, tossing a piece of food from the dish to Mochi.

"My child?"

"Yes. Your fur child. Unless you don't view him—-"

"No, I do. I just didn't think you would."

"I never did, but then I thought you couldn't have a genuine bond with anyone. I thought it was a lie, but Wren changed that."

"That's good news for me, then. I best thank my favorite little man for making his father available to me." I chuckled, leaning down and pressing a kiss to Wren's forehead. Stepping back, I went and got a drink and Marco scowled at me.

"You best not have just missed Wren and not me, Mr Grayson."

"If I did, what would you do about it, Mr Di Salvo?"

Marco set Wren in the high chair, made sure he was safe before he backed me into the counter, leaned down and let his lips brush my ear. "I'm keeping track. Don't think I'm not. I can't wait to drag every single orgasm out of you painfully slow and mind numbing. Four weeks, I should have plenty saved for then."

"You're just giving me something to look forward to, Marco. I'm counting down the time to when I can touch you. I want to devour you." I groaned, running my fingers down his chest.

"I could get you off right now, if you tell me how bad you need it." Marco whispered, pressing his lips to mine.

"Nope. If you want me to go to work, we can't do that or this. Or I will call in." I sighed.

Marco gave me space, and I hated it, but it was for the best. At least right now, while he was injured, when he was cleared for physical activities, that was an entirely different story.

After dinner, he gave me a long kiss. "Please be safe."

"I always do, Marco." I said, and he frowned.

"We both know that isn't true, or else we wouldn't have met," he said, and walked me to the front door. We reluctantly parted, and I headed off to work. I knew that as soon as I got done with work later, Marco would be waiting up for me.

Getting to work, Mia texted me to let me know she had called in with the flu, and to have a good shift without her. Sending her a text back, I asked her if she needed anything to help with her flu symptoms, and I would call her on break to check on her.

I got stuck with an EMT named Jared, and his paramedic partner was also off sick. He seemed pretty normal and down to earth. We got along fine. Our first call was for a car accident and we dealt with that quickly. Sitting in the passenger seat waiting for another call, I watched out the windshield at the darkness settling around us.

"I heard from a cop friend that there's a murder on the loose," he said, turning to look at me.

"And? Is it true?" I asked him, and he hummed.

"Most likely, the day crew was called to a scene for multiple victims. Only one of the three victims made it to the hospital."

"Shit. That's never a call you want to make. DOAs aren't a welcomed sight." I said, and silently prayed that we weren't in for a night like that.

Dispatch radioed in with a report of a male patient of unknown age with stab wounds. Jared wasted no time getting us on the way to the scene. The lights flashing, and the siren going. Neither of us really said anything more than necessary until we arrived on location.

Jared and I got out, getting everything we needed. A police car sat along the side of the road, and the officer had his hands covering wounds on the male. Getting gloves on, I set to work, stabilizing the man before getting him into the ambulance. Stuffing wounds with gauze and getting him onto the gurney, Jared and I were moving double time as our patient was losing blood faster than I could keep it in him.

The problematic wound was on his leg, and was still spilling out blood. Jamming my finger into the wound to halt the bleeding was doing the job I hoped. Jared got us there, and our patient changed from our hands into more capable ones.

Jared drove us back to the ambulance bay to clean our bus, and so I could get changed into clean and blood-free clothing. Taking a quick shower and cleaning myself off, I got dressed, Jared and I went back into the ambulance. We took the time to clean and sterilize our ambulance for the next call.

After a full night of bullshit, I sighed, heading up the walkway to Marco's. The door opened before I could even grab the door handle. Romeao stood there and spoke, "You look like shit."

"Long fucking shift." I groaned, feeling pretty dead on my feet. He closed the door behind us, and Marco was sitting at the table preparing a coffee. He looked up and stuck out the coffee to me.

"No, but I appreciate the offer."

"You look tired, Ambrose." Marco said, standing up and reaching out to pull me against him. "You smell odd."

"Cheap body wash." I muttered, wrapping my arms around him lightly and taking a deep breath of his spicy scent I adored.

"Would you like some food before you head off to sleep?" Romeao asked, sitting down and sipping his coffee. I shook my head and let go of Marco. Heading to the couch, I took my jacket and pants off, tossing them over the back of the couch. As far as I was concerned right now, my boxers and t-shirt were more than enough clothing to sleep in.

"Ambrose, go to the bedroom and sleep." Marco said, taking my clothing off the back of the couch. "Romeao and I have a couple people coming, work related. I want you to get proper sleep in my bed without us disturbing you."

"Ok." I muttered, getting up and heading to the bedroom. Mochi was sleeping in the bed on Marco's side, and he looked pretty comfortable there. Laying down beside him, he scooted closer, and I kissed the top of his head before passing out.

I woke up a few hours later, to Marco's deep voice telling someone else to keep it down and stop yelling before they woke me up. Stretching out on the bed, I listened to Marco chewing someone out. Giving it a few more minutes, I got out of bed, putting some sweatpants on and heading out to the living room.

Marco noticed me first as I yawned, stretching my hands over my head on the way to the kitchen to get coffee. My shirt rode up and Marco was on my tail, right to the kitchen. Romeao was gone, but I figured not for that long.

"Did they wake you?" he asked and grabbed a coffee cup for me, and filled it with coffee. He passed it to me.

Dressing up my coffee, I took a sip and groaned. "Nope. I got up naturally."

"Good. I was worried I might have to beat some sense into them. I still might if they look at you again."

"Hmm? What way did they look at me? I never noticed." I muttered, setting my coffee down on the counter and reaching out to pull Marco closer to me.

"When you stretched, your shirt rode up, and evidently I was not the only one watching the show." Marco hissed.

"Are you jealous that someone else looked at me?" I hummed.

"If I answer that honestly, we both would fear the answer, Ambrose."

"Don't worry. Mr Di Salvo, you are the only mafia man, and man for me. No one else compares." I chuckled, grabbing my coffee to take another sip of the sweet bean water of life. "You're more than welcome to tell them I am yours, Marco."

His hand slipped up the bottom of my t-shirt, and he spoke. "It's too late for you to run, Ambrose. You are mine, welcome or not. I enjoy you far too much to willingly let you go."

# 25 - Twenty - Five - Ambrose Grayson's Point Of View.

- - - - - - - - - - - - - - - - - - - - - - - - - - - - - - - - - - - - - - - - - - - - - -

Relaxing on the couch tucked into Marco's side, I watched Wren rolling around on the floor, playing by himself. I felt far too comfortable with this lifestyle now. I could see this as my complete future and be one hundred per cent alright with this. Looking at Marco, Mochi was behind his head on the back of the couch. It was funny because Mochi seemed to be as taken with Marco as I was.

This felt like home to me now.

"Ambrose, you look lost in thought."

"I was.. it was quite nice." I hummed and laid my head against his shoulder.

"What were you thinking about?"

"Oh, I was thinking about how this feels like home to me now. If that makes any sense to you."

"No, that makes total sense. I can't say I'm not pleased that you are finding a home here with Wren and I." He smiled and pulled me closer. I rested my head on his chest and listened to his heartbeat. I felt a sense of contentment and peace that I hadn't felt in a long time. None of this I thought was possible from a mafia man.

"I am hopelessly attached to Wren and you, Marco. Anything less than being here with you two is not good enough for me." I sighed, and he slipped his hand into my hair.

"Then stay with us for as long as possible," he whispered, and I smiled widely, feeling oddly full of joy and love.

"I will." I hummed and looked at Wren. He was asleep on the floor. "Do you want me to put him to bed?"

"No, you can leave him there. It won't hurt him to sleep there. He also might not go back to sleep if you move him." Marco said, as he slipped his hand underneath my shirt and down my hip.

"Marco." I hissed, and he gave me a sly smile.

"I was feeling a little better," he hummed, and rubbed my bare skin directly under his fingers.

"Are you done?"

"Hm. Nope. Just getting started actually," he chuckled.

"You are still injured." I bitched at him and tried to remove his hand.

"Ambrose I am being patient and understanding of you, and your care for my wound healing. But you're pushing it. If I don't at least get my hands on you like this, I might lose my sanity."

"So damn dramatic." I sighed, and I heard him click his tongue at me. "Well. Touch me, let's get this over with. But if you so much as complain about being in pain, or hurting, I'll give your damn ass a chastity belt."

"Stand up, I'm taking Wren to bed, then I'm coming for you, my sweet Ambrose." Marco whispered, his lips brushing against my ear and giving me shivers.

Standing up, Marco got up without my help and scooped Wren off the floor. He barely made a sound or movement in Marco's arms. I waited for Marco to return, baby monitor in hand.

"Come along Ambrose. We have a scheduled play time." Marco said, his eyes lit up almost like a kid in a candy store.

"Don't overdo it. I'm serious."

"You worry too much, carossimo."(Dearest)

"Mmm. You can speak dirty to me in Italian anytime." I hummed, following Marco to the bedroom. He turned to me after setting the baby monitor down on the dresser.

Sitting down on the bed, I looked up at Marco as he stalked closer to me, and set his hands on my chest and pushed me backwards onto the mattress. His hands resumed the delightful attack as he pushed my shirt up.

"Do hold this for me," he said, smiling as he lightly stuffed the hem of my shirt into my mouth to keep it in place. I grunted at him with my mouthful, and he seemed far too pleased with himself. He lifted my legs and took his time removing my pants and boxers.

Grunting at him again, I wanted to tell him to stop, but he gave me a look.

"Enough of that, Ambrose. I'm fine, just trust me, alright." I relaxed again, and he moved away from me, heading to the dresser. "Don't move."

He had a few things in his hands when. He came back, and I spotted the lube first. I would definitely stop him if he tried anything too rough. Penetration, giving or receiving, was too much for him.

He poured some of the lube into his hand and grabbed my semi hard cock. "This might be a little uncomfortable at first...but you should get used to it."

I looked down, confused, until finally confusion gave way to recognition. A cock ring. Marco had put a cock ring on me. With no kind of warning, the cock ring vibrated, and I jumped, letting out a groan. He was using his phone to adjust the level of vibration I was receiving.

Marco set the pace of the vibration and dropped his phone on the bed. His fingers grazed the head of my cock and I bit down on my shirt harder than before. Marco let his hands venture all over my skin while his present to me vibrated and had been touched with a vibrator before, but this was different. He moved his hands off me and undressed. Everything, even his boxers, were dropped to the floor. He crawled up onto me and sat down on-top of my cock and the ring as it pulsed away.

"Ooo. That's quite a strong vibration."

I tried to spit out the shirt, and he frowned at me. Leaning down, he gently pulled the shirt out of my mouth, and before I could utter words, he pressed his lips against mine and his tongue in my mouth. Marco's cock was rubbing against my lower stomach, and he was panting when he pulled his lips away from mine.

"Marco, you're injured. This isn't—" Marco shoved my shirt back into my mouth and smiled. "Hush."

I grunted at him and he reached for his phone. He experimented with it, and I grunted, my legs twitching from the vibrations. I bit down on my shirt hard when the cock ring pulsed the strongest yet, and I was convinced it was scrambling my brain cells. Wetness hit my chest, and my chin and I became momentarily aware of the pain on Marco's face before my mind numbing plummet towards an orgasm faded my surroundings.

Marco moved off me and turned the cock ring off. He took his sweet time taking the ring off me. Warmth and wetness covered the head of my cock. It was too much. I was so fucking sensitive that this small amount of touch made my hips jerk.

"Come now, relax. I'm just cleaning you up."

I let the shirt fall out of my mouth and hissed when Marco's tongue ran over the slit in my cock head. "Ugh! Too much."

"Hmm. You must be so sensitive after that," he basically purred at me, and I wanted to kiss him.

"Kiss me."

"Alright." he chuckled and pressed his lips to my cock before he wrapped his mouth around me. Plunging my overly sensitive cock into the warm, wet depths of his mouth. I tried to push him away, but he just wasn't going.

"Marco...ahh! Fuck please, I'm begging you, stop. I can't fuck you and this is too much."

He moved off my cock, and I took a deep breath, my body still jerking.

"This is just a taste of what I'm going to do to you the moment I'm cleared to have sex," Marco said, his fingers brushing my cock again.

"Marco." I bitched and reached out, pulling him down against me. "Kiss me, fuck."

Our lips met, and the kiss was tender. Marco ran his fingers through my hair and sighed. "I just want to make love—no, scratch that. I just want to have rough toe curling sex with you. I want to be the reason you can't think straight. I want to see you beg me, really beg me to stop."

Marco's face when he came. Pain clear on his features rocketed through my mind, and I frowned. "You were in pain, Marco. I told you not to overdo it. You could injure yourself even more."

"It was nothing. I could handle it," he said, and the soft smile on his face pissed me off. I wanted to fight with him about this, and he knew it.

"Chew me out about it another time, Ambrose. Don't run this time between us, right now."

Clenching my teeth, I let out a sigh. He was right. I didn't want to ruin this moment of closeness between us by bitching at him about his questionable pain tolerance.

"I'm going to check on Wren. Run us a shower, will you?" Marco said.

"Alright. Will do."

As soon as he left the room, after getting redressed, I followed suit and got dressed, tossing on my pair of boxers from before. Walking to the bathroom, I flicked the shower on and waited for Marco.

He strolled in a few minutes later and checked me out. "Wren is still out, and I gave Mochi food."

"That's why he likes you," I laughed, and waited till Marco pulled his t-shirt off. "Let me see your wound."

"My wound is fine. I would tell you if it wasn't."

"That's great. I'm glad. Even so, let me see your damn wound. I want to look for myself." I said. My voice was a little more demanding than I would have liked it to be. But then again, I was worried about him.

He sighed, but removed the gauze pad and his wound on the surface was almost gone. Underneath, however, there would definitely be damage still. He still had a while to heal up fully and re-strengthen his damaged muscles.

"You're healing well." I hummed, and brushed my fingers over the skin, closed but shiny.

"My body is a seasoned professional healing wounds like this."

"I hate that." I muttered, pulling the tape off his skin, since he could get the closed skin wet now. I wrapped my arms around him in a gentle hug and kissed the side of his neck. "I just want you to be safe, Marco."

# 26 - Twenty - Six - Ambrose Grayson's Point Of View.

V ibrating with anger, I tried my hardest not to be as angry as I was. But Marco was gone when I came home, and someone else was babysitting Wren. Not Romeao. I should have known when he wanted to fool around a week ago that he was testing the limits of what his body could handle. Instead, I ignored the red flag and now he was out working when he should rest still. He wasn't at all healed enough. Six to eight weeks was not enough to heal properly.

"You can leave, I've got Wren." I said to the enforcer, but he just smiled at me.

"I would love to leave early, but I can't. Marco asked me to stay until he got back himself so that you can rest after work."

"Oh." I said, biting my tongue so I wasn't rude to this man since it wasn't his fault Marco wasn't home. Heading to the bedroom, I opened the door, and my things cluttered the space. Looking around the room, I was a little more annoyed now. Why the hell was my stuff here?

The enforcer was on the couch, his phone in his hand, when I came out, and he looked at me.

"Excuse me, do you by chance know when Marco brought my things here, and where the rest of things went?" I asked.

"Marco had a few of us pack your things under his supervision last night, and he brought everything here. I believe most of your things are still in the garage."

"There's a garage?" I asked, having never actually seen it.

"Yes. There's a three-car garage behind the house with a loft above it."

"Well. That's news to me. But then, I haven't even seen the backyard." I said and turned back around to head back to the bedroom. Going around all my things, I laid in the bed beside Mochi after stripping down to my boxers and one of Marco's shirts.

I felt giddy about Marco bringing my things here, but at the same time, that scarred me. What if I messed up and had nowhere to go if he made me leave? Snuggling into Marco's pillow, I took a deep breath and closed my eyes. My long night was finally catching up with me.

Marco coming through the door sometime later was enough to wake me up, and the anger that I had come back to the surface when I heard Romeao and him speaking. Taking a deep breath, I got out of bed and pulled some sweatpants on before leaving the bedroom. Entering the kitchen, my coffee maker sat alongside his and Romeao was the first to say hello to me.

Marco greeted me. I nodded and sat down at the table. I wanted to bring up a few different things with him, but right now it probably wasn't smart with Romeao here.

"How was work?" Marco asked.

"It was work. Should I follow up and ask you how your day at work was, or would you like me to ignore that you're still injured?" I said flatly, some of my anger seeping out in my tone.

"We can discuss that later, Ambrose." Marco said politely, and I knew he rather not bring it up in front of Romeao.

"Then can you tell me why my things are in the bedroom and how they got here?"

"Right. I meant to send you a message to let you know, but I got side-tracked. There's increased police presence and canvassing because of the murders, and I wanted to keep you away from that. I would rather you and your things stay here with me," Marco said, and I frowned at him, even though I was actually thrilled to be here with him.

"Alright, that's understandable, thank you." I said, letting it go on this matter since it wasn't something that actually bothered me. "Oh right, before I forget. I have next week and a half off work. I had no choice but to use my paid vacation time, so I figured I could use the time to relax."

Marco smiled and slipped his hand on my thigh under the table. "Sounds good. It will be nice to have you here without having to send you to work."

"Have a good afternoon, you two. I have paperwork to do." Romeao hummed and left. I crossed my arms and looked at Marco.

"Ambrose, I understand you are probably mad at me about working, and moving your things here. But I had to. Trust me in that, at the very least. Please." Marco said, and I could see the sincerity in his eyes.

"I do trust you, Marco. That's why I'm still here, and not as mad about my things as you might think. I'm more mad about you going to work than anything. I'm really worried you're going to injure yourself when you're not even fully healed yet." I sighed and set my hand on his.

"I know you're worried. Believe me, I know. But I can't just sit here and heal. I don't have that luxury. I'm an underboss. I have far too much to do." Marco confessed.

Sighing, I understood. I really did, but it didn't mean that I liked it. But this was just how Marco was. There was a reason his ex-husband said he was my problem.

Marco got up and leaned over, pressing his lips to mine. "Let's do something as a family unit tomorrow."

I smiled, unable to stop myself. He called us a family unit. "I'd love that."

Hell, I would like that more than anything. To be a part of someone's family felt almost too good. I did not know when that had become a craving for me. I was never thinking about family before, never. This was completely new to me. I never once thought it was within my reach.

"Ambrose?"

I turned to look at him and wondered what I might say to explain these feelings I had now. "Yes?" I said, my voice barely audible. He stepped closer and put his hand on my shoulder.

"I hope I didn't make you uncomfortable by calling us a family unit. You've accepted me, and clearly Wren and I are a packaged deal, so um—-"

"I like it. To be completely honest, it makes me feel so good to hear you call us a family unit. I've never actually wanted a family unit, but I say that when I picture a family, it's this one." I confessed, cutting him off in the middle of his sentence. He smiled and pulled me into a hug. I could feel the warmth of his body against mine as we embraced. We stood like that for a few moments, and I felt a sense of belonging that I had never felt before. Not to say that I didn't feel like I belonged in my family.

Marco left to go check on Wren and brought him out to the living room just as I got out there myself. Marco tucked him into his play seat and went to get him the frozen teething ring from the freezer. Offering it to him, he took it and chewed on it.

"He really likes that ring you found him. I think he likes the feeling when he chews on it. Can't say I blame him, though the texture is quite satisfying."

Marco sat on the couch and beckoned me over. Sitting on the couch beside him, he pulled me down into this lap, and ran his fingers through my hair, while holding my head into his lap.

"I would have laid down and rested my head in your lap. You only had to ask." I chuckled and closed my eyes, enjoying the feeling of his fingers on my scalp and the heat radiating off his skin. I opened my eyes again and looked up at him. His gaze was warm and inviting, and he smiled at me. I leaned up and kissed him softly on the lips.

"Mmm." Marco hummed against my lips, and His tongue flicked out, plunging into the depths of my mouth, and stroking my tongue. "Your kisses are as addicting as always, Ambrose."

The allure of Marco's cologne clouded my thoughts, tempting me to succumb to my desires. My hands longed to explore his body, but deep down, I knew that acting on these impulses would be unwise. The fear of unintentionally causing him pain or harm during our intimate moments weighed heavily on my conscience. The guilt I would feel if my pursuit of pleasure resulted in his discomfort was something I couldn't bear.

"Please heal as fast as you possibly can, Marco. Keeping my hands off you is becoming a laborious task, as of late," I sighed, unable to resist the temptation any longer. With a gentle touch, I reached up and stroked the side of his cheek, feeling the warmth of his skin under my fingertips.

"Then don't. You can touch me, Ambrose, God. I want you to touch me. I need it." He said, and took my hand off his cheek and pressed it to his lips, planting kisses on my fingertips.

"I want you too, Marco." I said, pulling my hand back from him. "But we can't do this right now. You're still far too injured for this."

Marco refused to let me out of his lap. "Ambrose, I'm being patient with you about my wound, but I am growing tired of not being able to touch you."

"I would go back to my apartment to make this easier on both of us, but someone made that impossible to do." I bitched at him, some of my anger from earlier slipping through.

Marco took a deep breath, and I could tell that yelling at him had gotten under his skin a fair bit. Even so, the man still didn't let me go.

"I told you. It's too late now, Ambrose. I won't let you go."